Dead Girls Don't Love

Dead Girls Don't Love is published by Dragon's Roost Press.

Alive in the Wolf's Belly *Enchanted Conversation* December 2011
FawnGirl14 *Not Our Kind: Tales of (Not) Belonging* February 2015
The Cold Earth *Familiar Spirits* September 2015
Iceheart *Space!* June 2015
Invincible *Heroes!* March 2015
Sa fè lontan / Long Time, No See *That Hoodoo, Voodoo, That You Do* January 2015
Midnight Laundry *The Red Penny Papers* June 2011
Shadows of the Darkest Jade *Historical Lovecraft: Tales of Terror Through Time* April 2011
Saffron Skies *Time Traveled Tales, Volume 2* September 2014
Frozen Souls *Candle In the Attic Window* September 2011
The Smoking Nun *EGM Shorts* November 2015
When The Stars Are Right *Eldritch Embraces: Putting the Love back in Lovecraft* February 2016
Dead Girls Don't Love *Still Hungry For Your Love* November 2013

Printed in the United States of America

First Printing, 2018

ISBN-13: 978-0-9988878-4-5
ISBN-10: 0-9988878-4-6

Dragon's Roost Press
207 Gardendale
Ferndale, MI 48220

http://thedragonsroost.net/styled-3/index.html

2018

Dead Girls Don't Love

by

Sarah Hans

DEDICATION

To Scott, My First Reader

TABLE OF CONTENTS

Introduction

Thank you for buying or borrowing this book, and thank you for reading the introduction. Nobody ever reads introductions! So I'll try to keep it short and entertaining.

I've wanted to be a genre writer for as long as I can remember. When I was 18 years old, I sent off a story to a now-defunct fantasy magazine. When my story was returned covered in red ink, I naively thought that meant I was a terrible writer and I stopped writing short stories almost completely. I turned to other creative pursuits (mainly roleplaying games) and let my dream of being a writer wither on the vine.

But fate intervened. Nearly ten years later, I met a guy at a convention who would end up becoming one of my closest friends. That guy, writer/publisher/ paladin Steven Saus, inspired me to start writing short stories with the intent of having them published--and being paid for it. I looked at calls for anthologies to give me something to write about, and the first story I wrote was "Shadows of the Darkest Jade," included in this collection. Luckily for me, that story sold to the amazing (and now unfortunately out of print) anthology

Historical Lovecraft. The second story I wrote also sold. And the third.

I wasn't getting paid much. Most of these early venues paid only one cent a word, which most writers wouldn't bother with. The advice I've gotten in the years since, as I've become more and more serious about my writing career, is to avoid venues that pay small amounts. But I consider myself lucky that I didn't try for a professionally paying market right out of the gate, because if I had, I wouldn't have experienced that first taste of success, and the second, and the third. I might have given up again. I might have turned back. This collection wouldn't exist without those early successes to boost my confidence. I needed the confidence more than I needed the money, in the beginning.

If you're a writer, or an artist, or whatever your aspirations are, don't let anyone tell you there's only one way to do it. Back away slowly from anyone who tells you there's a singular path to success, or even only one way to define success. You are the captain and the navigator on your ship, and you get to determine whether you sail for the stars or the moon. That can be terrifying and frustrating--who doesn't long for the days when the path to success was laid out by high school guidance counselors and college deans--but it's also liberating. It's powerful. It's how you really live.

Don't measure your success by someone else's

metric, or by their timeline. And don't stop doing what you love because someone else believes you're not doing it "the right way." Listen to the people who have achieved what you want to achieve, and consider their advice, but always remember: the adventure is yours alone.

The fact I have a collection of fiction (An actual book! Of my own stories!) to place in the hands of readers is proof that what you need is to be a successful writer is just to write. It's not about talent, as I mistakenly assumed when I was a teenager; it's about perseverance. It's about dedication. It's about tenacity and a willingness to learn. It's also about making friends with publishers and knowing when their blood-alcohol ratio is such that when you pitch them your collection, they'll say yes...but, I digress.

If I can get to this point, so can you. I believe in you. Now read this book, and every time you think "I could write a better story than that," I dare you to do it. I don't deserve to have a collection more than you do. I'm just a chick who wrote enough stories to fill a book.

Go on, get on with it. And thanks again.

-Sarah

Alive in the Wolf's Belly

Being eaten alive by the wolf was the best thing that ever happened to me. It was also the worst.

The story goes that when he knocked on my front door I was so myopic or senile I thought he was Jenny, my granddaughter. But my eyesight, and my mind, have never been keener.

That's the scandalous truth: I knew all along I was letting the wolf into my parlor.

There was a moment, after he knocked, when I shuffled to the door and heard his heavy breathing on the other side, I remember well: A moment of decision. The porch creaked under his weight. The scent of his musky fur wafted in through the cracked window. I looked through the peephole and saw his huge, black eyes, peering back at me.

I thought about my life. I thought about the endless afghan I was crocheting, the tea steeping on the stove that I made each day in the hopes of a visit from children or grandchildren who rarely bothered, the loneliness since my husband had died six years before.

And then I opened the door.

The wolf was bigger than I could have imagined.

He flowed into the room and filled it with his bulk. He brought with him the scent of the forest, and the mysteries of the shadows were close on his heels. He was a creature older and greater than I could comprehend.

His eyes as he regarded me were not full of malice, as you might think. They were wise, intelligent eyes...but they were hungry.

He opened his mouth and I smelled the sickly-sweet scent of fresh blood and chewed meat. His great jaw touched the floor, and I climbed into his mouth, as one would mount the steps of a carriage, using his fangs as hand-holds. Once I was comfortable on his tongue, his jaws snapped shut, and I was swallowed whole.

Encased in darkness, I was squeezed into the creature's gullet, and from there his stomach, where I rested in a pool of acid. It was painful and horrible and wonderful all at once. It reminded me of birthing my daughters, when the pain was so intense that it seemed to consume the world, and my focus became a needle-sharp point. All the loneliness and sadness and bitterness was swept away in a wash of pain.

And then the creature roared, and I was jostled, and then a great split appeared, spilling light into the tight darkness of the beast's stomach. Two pairs of hands reached in and pulled me out, into the light.

Jenny and the huntsman poured water over me and scrubbed the acid from my skin. I trembled and wept. They wrapped me in Jenny's red cloak and put me in bed with a cup of tea steaming on the nightstand.

The next morning I found that the wolf's carcass had been taken away, all except the head. The huntsman wanted to take that too, but I told him I wanted it. He gave me an odd look, but as so often happens, I got my way, because it's excusable to be a bit eccentric when you're my age.

The wolf's head is mounted on my wall. I wish I had his skin, so I could wrap myself in it, but I make due. The floors are still stained red with his blood, and on those lonely nights when no one visits me, and the acid burns on my legs itch, I curl naked on the floor beneath his massive jaws and remember what it was like to be alive.

FawnGirl14

Papa borrowed the neighbor's hand saw to remove my antlers less than a day after I returned home. He mumbled as he sawed: What kind of doe has antlers anyway? Never heard of such a thing.

She's special, Mama told him. Our special girl. Of course she has antlers. Mama tried to smile proudly at me, but her eyes filled with tears.

I didn't protest. I had to turn sideways to fit through doorways; my neck ached, unable to bear the burden. I couldn't be seen in public with antlers, so they had to go. Still, once they were gone, I missed their weight. Papa threw them in the trash. Mama, who must have seen the look in my eyes when Papa discarded a part of me so casually, rescued them later after he passed out in his recliner. She wrapped them in grandmere's shawl and brought them to me, wiping at my tears with her fingertips. We will treasure every part of you, she whispered, pulling me into her warm embrace, stroking my downy fur. We will never let any part of you go again.

As she hugged me tight, I believed her with the naiveté of a teenager. I had been gone forty years, but I had been gone only four days. I was fourteen and fifty-four, all at once. I knew how to survive the thicket, but I didn't know about the world. I was a girl, and I was also...something else. Something transformed.

My parents were transformed too, of course. I barely recognized them, paunchy in places they hadn't been forty years ago, faces creased with wrinkles and hair frosted with white. Even the house was different, the pumpkin carpets replaced with beige, the avocado walls now a neutral shade of brown. The fluffy sofa upholstered in flowers had been replaced with a sleek, black leather model, cold and smooth to the touch and smelling faintly of death.

The only room in the house unchanged was my bedroom, still decorated with pink rosebuds and unicorn figurines. I slept on the floor, the bed too soft and confining, and woke at every sound, fearing that the barking of the neighbor's dog was the braying of the Huntsman's hounds, that Papa's footsteps on the stair were the Huntsman's booted tread. Every night, I dreamed the same dream: I snuck out to meet a boy whose name I could no longer remember, creeping through the woods behind our house to meet him without even a flashlight. Clandestine. Every night, I tripped on a root in the darkness and skinned my knee. And every night, the Huntsman found me, and I woke trembling, thrashing, tangled in my blankets and covered in a thin sheen of sweat.

One week to the day of my return, a family of deer appeared in the yard during breakfast. They nibbled the soft buds of Mama's crocuses that poked out of the snow. My mouth watered. Mama and I watched them in silence until Papa stomped into the kitchen, still groggy. Damn deer, he growled. Always eating the plants.

Then he froze, exchanged a glance with Mama, and quietly retreated from the room with no apologies, no explanations. Mama drew her arm around me. I wished she smelled like the loamy forest floor instead of soap and perfume, a thought I instantly regretted. The neighbor's dog barked and the deer fled into the woods. I tried not to pull away from the arms of the woman who birthed me.

A few weeks later, at Mama's funeral, Papa tried to tell me it wasn't my fault. She was sick before you returned. She'd been sick a long time.

He didn't say it, but I knew she'd been sick since I disappeared. The dagger-sharp stares of the mourners told me all I needed to know. Mama had died of grief. She would have been better off had I never returned. Then, at least, she could have pretended to move on, could live a life. It was a life with a dull ache in her chest, the loss of a child forever seared on her soul, but it was a life nonetheless.

Returning to her like this, as this creature, this

monster, this thing. That was what killed her. She took one look at me and knew her daughter was truly lost to her, forever. She had no reason to hope, no reason to go on.

Without Mama, Papa had no reason to go on, either. He lasted a year before cirrhosis took him. There was no funeral, just a hole in the backyard in which I buried his ashes. When the burying was done, I sat in his threadbare lawn chair, watching the shadows of deer milling in the forest at dusk and drinking the last of his whiskey in tribute. The whiskey tasted like poison, but it burned away the hard edges of my sorrow.

As the moon rose, I stripped off my clothes and stumbled drunkenly into the woods. My families were lost to me, both the family that had birthed me as a human child and the family that had rebirthed me as a creature of the hunt, but maybe I could have a new family. Branches caught at my hair and brambles snagged my skin. The deer regarded me warily until I drew too close, and then leaped away, gone in a flash, leaving me sobbing on the forest floor, naked, thin rivulets of blood decorating my skin.

In the distance, hounds howled. I ran home, my heart thundering, and took the longest, hottest shower of my life. I cleaned every nick and scrape with rubbing alcohol and wrapped myself in an entire roll of gauze. I locked all the doors and turned out all the lights and prayed that, this time, the hunt would pass me by.

When the sun rose again and I was still myself, still a girl with antlers and dead parents and a house she couldn't afford—not even with Papa's social security check, which I still received, because, per his instructions, I'd never reported his death—I turned my attention to more practical matters. Papa had known death was coming for him, so he tried to teach me how to cope before he left. Taught me how to use the computer, the internet, the debit card. Tried to help me find work. I'd been declared dead thirty-five years ago, and without a birth certificate or a social security card honest work was hard to come by. I filed down my perpetually sprouting antlers, wore a hat, and marched to the farmer's market, where I cut fruit for cash a few hours each day.

My fruit-cutting often lured a crowd. Truth be told, it wasn't the fruit-cutting that attracted people. Unless you stood very close, it was difficult to see that my skin was so luminous because I was covered in a glossy layer of pale brown fur. My eyes were so enchanting because they were the eyes of a doe, ever wide and alert. My limbs were so slim and movements elegant because they were honed and trained by the long days of running and leaping on an agility course where failure meant death. I was a creature out of myth, a monster out of legend, and even if they couldn't quite understand how they knew, people could sense it.

It is miserable to be adored for the qualities you most despise.

You really know how to sell fruit, the vendor told me, handing me a wad of cash each afternoon and shaking his head in wonderment. I went home at two o'clock because the fruit was gone by then, whole truckloads of it. Other vendors tried to lure me away from the fruit stand, promising higher wages, shorter hours. But the idea of cutting meat made me feel dizzy, the idea of peeling shrimp made bile boil in my stomach. I loved the sweet-spicy smell of pears each morning, the crisp crack of rhubarb as my knife did its work. So, I stayed at the fruit stand.

Men wearing suits and flashy smiles gave me business cards, urged me to call them, because I was the fresh face they were looking for. I put their business cards in the bin with the peels and seeds. I shook my head at them and didn't try to explain that I was hiding from the hunt. Exposure and fame were the last things I wanted.

Security had to remove a few of my most persistent admirers. They had to call the police on one in particular. You could be famous, he screamed as they dragged him away in handcuffs. You could be rich.

As if those things would be worth attracting the attention of the Huntsman. As if money could deter his hounds.

And then there was Ian. I smelled him before I

saw him, a pungent aroma that made my nostrils clamp shut and my pulse beat a hard rhythm. He sidled up to me at the fruit stand and slipped a business card into the pocket of my juice-smeared apron. Call me if you need some help with your cash flow, he purred. Our kind have to stick together.

I thought but didn't say that he wasn't my kind. I left the card in my apron. I couldn't stand to touch it, not even to throw it away. Or maybe I was so shocked that I'd met someone else scarred by the thicket, I couldn't discard the evidence of that meeting, however repugnant it was to me.

The money from the fruit stand wasn't enough. Eventually, all the utilities were shut off. I didn't mind in the summer, as I preferred to sleep in the yard anyway. But as fall stretched toward winter, it became clear that soon there would not be enough blankets in the world to keep me warm, especially as I came home earlier and earlier from the fruit stand each day, the sheaf of money in my pocket slimmer and slimmer. That's the nature of seasonal work, the fruit vendor told me with a shrug. Not my problem.

I was lonely, too, I confess. The house was full of shadows. Shadows of my parents, shadows of the girl I'd once been. The fruit stand customers were friendly, but not friends. No one could understand the creature I had become, the monster I saw in the mirror each day, not quite human, not quite animal. No one except Ian.

I'll pay for the electricity, baby girl, Ian assured me. I'll pay for everything. And you'll never have to file your antlers again.

My customers started off few and far-between. They didn't ask for anything too bizarre. Most were willing to pay just to talk to FawnGirl14 over the internet, from the safety of their homes. Soon I had regular customers, regular appointments. Ian complimented me on how well I pretended interest in the lives of far-away men.

I didn't tell him I wasn't pretending. I didn't tell him they were the only human contact I had each day, cocooned in my warm house, and that I looked forward to each appointment, relished each contact. I ordered groceries by delivery and covered my head in hats, a turban, then a towel, and then, eventually, I asked that the groceries be deposited on the back porch, so I wouldn't have to see the delivery drivers at all. The more my online friendships grew, the further I was isolated.

My dreams grew more vivid. I woke each morning with a throat hoarse from screaming, the echoes of the Huntsman's horn resounding in my ears.

As my antlers grew in, customers asked me to touch them, rub them, apply lotion to them. Soon men wanted me to touch my private parts while they watched via webcam, but I declined them. Those are paying customers, Ian scolded. You do what they ask. Whatever they ask.

I refused. Ian threatened to shut down my profile, shut off my lights, turn off my heat. You will do as I say, or you will have nothing. You will be nothing.

I stood in the yard at dawn and watched the deer in the forest, nibbling at whatever greenery they could find in the snow. My legs throbbed with the urge to run. Hounds brayed in the distance and my heart thumped hard against my ribcage.

The men broke into my house on the first day of spring. Ian led them, his smile a leer of pointy teeth. They held me down with a knife pressed against my throat. Your kind are always so stupid, Ian hissed, his eyes flashing green. The Huntsman will find you eventually. He always finds you grazers. You're too stupid not to stay in one place, too docile not to keep him guessing.

I didn't weigh my options—I didn't have to. I calmly pressed my flesh against the knife until I felt the skin split, the blood ooze. I grinned at Ian and his comrades and they hesitated. Why is she smiling? That's just creepy, man. What the fuck is wrong with this chick?

The blast of the Huntsman's horn made them scramble. What the fuck was that? Sounded like a train. No, louder than a train.

More deadly than a train, too, I assured them, sliding from their slackened grips. My eyes never left

Ian's, so I saw the look of horror on his face as he studied the blood staining my collar.

Now that you've heard the hunt, you're doomed, fellas. You're prey.

Ian turned to run, but it was too late. The Huntsman didn't use doors. He didn't knock or ask permission to enter. He was in the house, around the house, everywhere. Hounds shrieked and spectral deer scattered before him like leaves on the wind.

You bitch, Ian screamed as an arrow pierced him through the chest. He reached for me, but the hounds scented his blood and swarmed him. He disappeared into a teeming mass of fur and teeth.

I rose, the commingled scents of fear and the loamy forest floor filling my lungs. I reveled in terror and comfort all at once. Love and hate, need and desire, a reason to live and a reason to die. As the herd swept past, I leapt eagerly to join them. The hounds nipped at my flanks. I ran and vaulted and danced, the Huntsman's spear narrowly missing my rump.

The mantra of the Wild Hunt filled my ears and I joined the song with a voice both my own and not: I am a creature of wind and grass and freedom. The Huntsman is my master and my liberator, and I am his eternally. I run so that he may chase, and he chases so that I may run.

So has it always been, and so shall it always be.

The Cold Earth

My husband, Tom, killed me on the first of May, angry because I overcooked the meatloaf. It was the last straw for both of us. When he grabbed my hair and slammed my head against the kitchen counter, I thought about how I had known for years this would be my inevitable end. Nobody survives living with a psychopath.

Tom buried me in the backyard beneath the old oak tree, where we'd shared our first kiss when I was only a blushing girl of seventeen. Even in death, I could still feel his hot breath on my face, his hands skimming my supple young body, the urgency of his erection pressed against my hip, as if it were happening at that very moment. I called out to the younger me, tried to warn her, but she just went right on kissing him.

My grave was cold beneath the oak, under the earth. My flesh melted away and my meat was eaten by worms. The tree's roots tickled my bones, wrapping around me in a woody embrace.

Mama never liked Tom. She wouldn't let us marry, so we eloped against her wishes the day I turned eighteen. Mama refused to speak to me after that. She was never a nice woman, not generous with a smile or a hug or even a kind word, but now I think maybe she did try to protect me, in the end. Maybe she did love me.

She died about a year after we eloped, killed by her two-pack-a-day habit, so we moved into the old farmhouse. It was convenient since Tom had lost his job and we were about to be evicted. He wouldn't let me work to help make ends meet. He said no wife of his would hold a job, like the concept was dirty and repulsive. I thought that was romantic, I thought he wanted to provide for me and take care of me. Wasn't that sweet? I didn't see that he was trying to control me. I didn't understand that he was cutting me off from the rest of the world and keeping me dependent on him. I didn't realize until things got bad.

Without a job, Tom turned to a life of crime. At first, he told me he was working third shift at the sandpaper factory in town. One day at the grocery store, one of the few places I was allowed to go alone, I overheard two women talking about how hard the factory closing was on their families. I confronted Tom about the lie and he hit me for the first time. Just once, on the face, just a slap, but hard enough to leave a handprint for a few days.

I packed my things and went to a friend's place. Tom came after me. He apologized. He brought me flowers. He told me he'd never hit me again. He promised things would be different, better. I was naive and silly and went back to him.

And things were better, for a while. But soon he was bringing suspicious packages home, hiding stolen cars in the barn, filing the serial numbers off firearms in the living room. My protests fell on deaf ears. He kept the only set of car keys. He canceled the phone service. My once-a-week visits to the grocery store were my only opportunity to see other people, and those were closely guarded. I became a prisoner.

I tried walking to town, once, and got picked up by a couple of Tom's "colleagues" halfway there. They took me home. Tom locked me in the root cellar for two days in punishment and then made me burn all my shoes. I never tried to run away again.

Those days were full of so much turmoil, so many hot tears, so much fear, so much hatred. Now, below the ground, it's cool and dry and my fear is replaced by the wisdom of the earth, the songs of trees, the whispered secrets of twining roots and digging beetles. Up above, the living scurry and rush, but down here we grow and decay and wait.

I am the worms that devour my flesh, the roots that coil about my bones. I am the cool night breeze and the warm summer soil. I am forgotten and at peace.

But then I hear a voice. A woman's voice. Laughing. I am her, and she is me, flirting with Tom beneath the oak tree. He murmurs something, he smiles. He stands on my grave and seduces her with promises. *I have money, baby girl, I have a whole house.* He can protect her, he can care for her. She's as young as I was when we first met, slim as a willow, breasts like mosquito bites and hip bones jutting into his hands as he touches her, persuading her with caresses and kisses. He's kind and attentive and charming, oh so charming, with that white smile and those blue, blue eyes.

My heart hurts, even though it was devoured by worms months ago. Emotions rush into the empty space that once was me. I have no throat to scream my pain, no lips to make words, but it's too much. I can't watch him do this all over again. The earth groans, the oak tree sways, and a branch tears away from the trunk without warning, crashing to the ground below. Tom dances out of the way and the branch narrowly misses the girl, who squeaks in alarm.

They laugh in relief and he puts his arm about her possessively, protectively, pulling her toward the house. He turns and looks back at the tree as they mount the porch and I see a flicker of recognition in his eyes.

Fear races through me, stinging like that first slap to my cheek. He knows I'm down here. He knows that branch was sent for him. I shrink back into the cool embrace of my grave, trying to will myself into nonexistence. I am dirt and worms and roots now. I am nothing. If I forget myself, then maybe he'll forget me, too.

Days and weeks pass in the darkness beneath the oak tree. Tom forgets about the branch, forgets about me again. The girl moves into the farmhouse with him. I don't want to hear their voices, but I do; even through six feet of soil, I can hear them laughing, making plans, making love. If I had ears, I'd pack them full of dirt, but I don't, so there's no way to block the two of them out. I draw the tree's roots tighter around my skeleton, sinking deeper into the earth, trying to find an end for this nightmare.

Winter comes, and I get some respite. The voices are muffled now that Tom and his new bride spend most of their time indoors and the plants that serve as my eyes and ears doze in hibernation.

I hear my name, *Megan*, and the sound rouses me from slumber. Tom's friends have gathered around a bonfire in the yard, not far from my resting place. *Jessica's a real pretty girl. Don't know how you keep getting women that good looking, Tommy. That Megan was a fine piece of ass, too. Whatever happened to her?*

None of your damn business.

Rage courses through me, cold as ice and hot as a brand. The oak's roots lash beneath me in response. I seek the heat of the fire, pushing at the earth. The men shout as the bonfire bursts apart, embers flying and burning logs rolling out of the fire ring. Someone shrieks, and I can smell the gut-churning stench of searing human flesh. The others tackle him with a blanket and put out the flames. He groans. *My leg, my leg!*

Christ, his jeans are melted to his skin. Someone call 9-1-1!

No! What're you thinking? We got a barn full of hot cars. Drive him to the hospital your damn selves.

They trundle the injured man into a car. I hear the sounds of many car doors slamming, engines revving, and then a fleet of cars and motorcycles drives off the property. Left behind, Tom curses and shouts, kicking at the smoldering logs and abandoned beer bottles. Jessica tries to calm him, telling him it'll be okay. She convinces him to go back inside and get some sleep.

The cold, blissful silence of winter snaps back into place the next morning and stays that way for another month. Then, the ground thaws. Rain falls instead of snow. Seeds begin to germinate, pushing new life into the soil. Wriggling worms breed in my eye sockets and fresh roots visit my earthy hideaway, humming the cheerful songs of green things growing.

Jessica decides to take up gardening, so Tom brings her seeds and flowers. She kneels in the yard, pulling weeds and hoeing the earth, dropping in seeds and patting the soil over them. She's very tender, very sweet, singing Guns 'n Roses love ballads to the sprouting plants and walking barefoot through the grass.

She and Tom get in a fight one night when he pours a bottle of beer over her garden. He locks her out of the house. She curls up on the porch, sobbing, one hand over her throbbing jaw. I remember the sharp pain of a fresh bruise as it blossomed purple across my face. She is me and I am her. She is too tender, too kind, too young for this. It took Tom several years to be this cruel to me, and they've been married for barely one. He'll kill her soon, like he did me, without even meaning to do it. And then her body will join mine, and we'll be together, sisters in death, the roots pressing us into a cool, final caress of bone on bone.

I'm lonely, but not lonely enough to watch Tom murder again.

I can save the girl yet.

The trees sway and rattle. The flowers tremble and whisper. Jessica sits up and looks at her garden.

Jessssssiiiiiicaaaaaaaaa.

She scrambles to her feet and runs to the door, pounding on it with her fists, shrieking and wailing. Floorboards creak as Tom moves through the house. The door opens and his fist thrusts out, catching her on the cheek, sending her tumbling back to the porch.

Please, Tommy, please don't leave me out here. It's haunted!

He pauses in the open door. *What'd you say?*

She sobs, hysterical, clutching at the porch railing as if it's a lifeline. *There's a ghost. It called my name.*

Tom strides out of the house, across the porch, to the barn. He returns with two shovels, presenting one to Jessica. He leads her to the oak tree and gestures to the place where he buried me. *Dig,* he says.

I should feel afraid. He's coming for me, again, one final time. But as they move the rain-softened soil away from my bones, I welcome them. What can he do to me in death, after all, that is worse than what he did to me in life? The earth is my flesh now, every tree and bush and blade of grass an extension of my ghostly body. I have power in death I did not possess in life.

Are . . .are those bones?

Keep digging. We need to get the whole skeleton.

Who is this, Tommy? Who did you bury? Is it Megan? Did you kill her?

Stop asking questions and dig, girl, if you don't want to hear no more ghost voices.

No. I won't keep going unless you tell me what happened. Who is this?

Tom raises his fist and lunges toward Jessica. My rage rushes up the oak tree and snaps another of its branches. The branch falls between them, hitting Tom's upraised arm. He bellows in pain.

Jessica scrambles for the edge of the hole while Tom is distracted. The soil is slippery and she's panicking,

unable to gain purchase. I command the roots that are
my fingers to make a ladder for her. She gasps for a
moment, unable to comprehend what she's seeing as the
roots intertwine before her very eyes.

Growling, Tom reaches for her again. She squeaks
and scales the ladder, kicking away Tom's groping fingers.
Tom tries to follow her up the ladder, but the roots
retract as soon as Jessica is safe. He slides down the side
of the hole and collapses, flailing, onto my skeleton.

The tree branches scratch and scrape together to
make the sound of my terrible laughter.

I command the roots to lift me. My corpse slides
from beneath Tom, rising up in the air high above him,
above the hole in the earth. The moon bathes me in
her silvery glow, illuminating my clean-picked bones
wrapped in roots, coiled with worms, dropping beetles
from above. My grin is white and menacing. The tarp in
which Tom buried me trails behind me like a dark veil,
fluttering and snapping in the breeze.

Until death do us part, the grasses whisper.

Jessica screams. Tom curses my name. The roots
which are my arms reach up and close around him,
pulling him down into the cool embrace of the grave.

Jessica plants hyacinths over my grave so I can
enjoy their sweet perfume every spring. She visits the
oak often to sit beneath its creaking branches. She talks

to me, telling me about the life growing in her belly, the postman she's going to marry, and the family she plans to have so she can fill the farmhouse with laughter and love as it should be.

She teaches her children to swing on a tire swing from the oak's branches. The children dig holes in the earth to whisper their secrets and longings to the oak's roots. I cradle them in my branches and protect them from sudden storms beneath my canopy.

When Jessica's eldest daughter is sixteen, a boy driving a mustang arrives to take her on a date. Jessica walks out to the oak tree to lean against my trunk, pressing her forehead to my rough exterior as she has so many times before.

She wipes tears from her cheeks. *I don't like this boy, Mother Megan. He reminds me of Tommy.*

Tom writhes and gurgles at the sound of his name, but the oak's roots coil more tightly about him, like a constrictor squeezing her prey, until he silences.

I don't like the boy either.

Iceheart

White Buffalo Outpost was deserted when Lola and I arrived to investigate their radio silence. Even the mining crew's thermal suits were missing from the mud room.

"Where could they have gone?" Lola asked, gesturing to the empty compartments where six suits should have rested.

"They probably had cabin fever and went for a stroll," I replied, stripping off my own suit and pushing it into a vacant compartment.

"I suppose we've seen worse." Lola slid out of hers and shoved it into the compartment beside mine.

"Isolation does strange things to people."

"Don't we know it. I'll check the living quarters. You got command?"

"See you in five."

We turned and ventured in opposite directions down the narrow corridor, just as we had dozens of times before over a decade of rescue missions.

The command center should have been bustling with activity, but instead I found the room silent, lights blinking automatically without human eyes to see them, a few motes of dust drifting in the air, stirred up by my boots. It smelled sterile, abandoned, as if the crew had never even existed. The outpost's desertion resonated.

I fiddled with the comm station controls, trying to get a signal through to our ship. After checking every frequency, I gave up and collapsed into the captain's chair. "Computer: captain's logs."

"Authorization required."

"Daniel Teegan, Native Mining Authorization two-six-eight-five-one."

"Thank you, Mister Teegan."

The crew's captain appeared before me, large as life. He was a tall man, with a craggy face, brown skin, black hair. I felt a pang of jealousy for his Lakota features and hated myself for still feeling such a petty emotion, even after all these years, even at my age.

The captain's voice was deep and monotonous as he discussed the conditions on the outpost. I was exhausted after a week of sleepless nights since Lola announced her engagement to my rival. Warm and comfortable, I let the captain's droning voice lull me into dozing.

"Dan!"

I sat up, suddenly very awake. Had I heard someone calling my name, or dreamed it? Blinking sleep from my eyes, I glanced at the clock on the display. Lola and I had separated almost half an hour ago. That felt like a long time. What could be keeping her? White Buffalo Outpost was small—only five rooms, really.

I heard another sound, this time a crashing, and then a shout. No words, just a grunted sort of scream.

The emergency weapons locker under the command console was empty but for a flare gun. "Wosiliyagle," I muttered. Where was the standard-issue pistol? The flare gun would be worse than useless in such close quarters, but the thought of venturing into the unknown unarmed was worse. I slipped the flare gun and three flares into the pockets of my coveralls before leaving the command center.

"Lola?" I called, inching down the corridor. Silence had fallen over the outpost again, and I strained to hear anything that might give me a clue. By the time I reached the door at the end, the one leading to the living quarters, my heart was pounding, making the blood rush in my ears. I licked my suddenly very dry lips and pressed the button on the wall.

The door hissed open, but the lights didn't come up automatically. A foul smell hit me and I covered my nose with my free hand. "Lola?" I called again. I stood in the doorway for a few heartbeats, waiting for something to happen.

Lola came screaming toward me from out of the darkness. Her face was a rictus of pain and terror. Her arms, her legs, her face, everything was covered in blood.

She barreled into me and took us both to the floor, where she struggled to rise, clawing at me in panic.

"Lola! It's me, it's Dan! What happened?" I tried to grab her as she scrambled away from me and down the hall toward the command center. I chased after her. She dove under the console.

I knelt down under the console to get to her. "Where are you hurt?" When I tried to touch her, she screamed and backed away, clutching at her neck. Blood pumped out between her fingers. Her eyes were so wide she looked like a terrified doll. "Let me get the first aid kit," I told her, but when I turned away, she grabbed my wrist and held me. I let her pull me in close. Her other hand came away from her neck and drew my face down to hers, smearing blood across my jaw. The uncovered wound was long and ragged, a second mouth that oozed blood.

She whispered only one word: "Wendigo."

She released me. I went for the first aid kit. She didn't protest or struggle when I pulled her from under the console so I could inject her with pain killers, apply coagulants, bandage her neck. My hands shook as I worked, and I talked to myself under my breath, trying to keep myself calm. Sweat poured down my forehead, obscuring my vision, and I wiped it away, smearing more blood across my face. My vision narrowed to a tunnel, and at the end of that tunnel was Lola. Her attacker was still on the station, somewhere, but I couldn't worry about him. Lola was all that mattered. All that had ever mattered.

When I was done, I sat down on the floor beside her in the disturbingly large pool of blood. The command center smelled like a butchery. "You're going to be okay, Lola."

Her eyes rolled up to look at me though the rest of her remained immobile. Green eyes, startling in contrast with the brown of her skin and the black of her hair, even more notable now with her skin so unnaturally pale. Lola Spotted Tail, the Oglala girl with green eyes. "You Blackfoot are such bad liars," she rasped.

I pressed my fingers to her lips, unable to suppress a relieved chuckle. She was well enough to make sarcastic remarks, which made the fist inside my chest unclench just a little. And she had referred to me as Blackfoot, which gave me that tingly all-over warm feeling it always did. Lola had never cared that I didn't look like one of The People. Maybe that was why I loved her. That, and the sarcasm.

"I'd tell you not to talk, but I know you Oglala aren't good at following orders," I quipped.

Lola gave a strained smile but didn't speak again. Fear shadowed her normally bright eyes.

"I'm going to call for help," I said, giving her hand a squeeze and getting up. I tried not to notice that her fingers were cold, too cold, and sticky with blood.

I went to the comm station and twirled dials, trying every frequency again. "This is Daniel Teegan at White Buffalo Outpost. SOS. SOS. Please respond."

Static was the only answer.

"We must be out of range," I told Lola, kneeling beside her again and clasping her hand in mine. "We have to get off the station, off Inyan, back to base. Nobody's coming to help. Can you walk? Never mind, I can carry you."

I hooked my arm under her shoulders and drew her to standing. Her legs wobbled and she collapsed into the captain's chair, shaking her head. Her eyes rolled about, unfocused, and her mouth moved, but she made no sound beyond a gurgle. Blood frothed on her lips.

"Get up, get up *now*," I ordered. I wanted to sound authoritative but my voice shook too much. I only managed to sound scared. I put my hands on her shoulders and yanked her from the chair. Hauling her toward the door, I was grateful that she had been chosen for this mission, because any of the other rescue squad members would have been too big for me to carry this way. A punch of guilt hit me so hard I had to stop walking for a moment, the breath knocked from my lungs. If I hadn't requested her as my partner, Lola wouldn't have been here in the first place. She wouldn't have been attacked, wouldn't now be staring over the precipice of death.

I couldn't let her die. I couldn't face a life without Lola, a life wracked with guilt. If Lola died, I would die too. Maybe not here on this station, but by inches, every day, until I was a ghost. She had to live.

These were the thoughts that gave me enough strength to get us both to the mud room. I lowered Lola gently onto the bench beside our thermal suits.

"You're nearly as pale as I am," I told her, hoping to get a smile, but she didn't even look at me. I took down a thermal suit and lifted her feet into it. "You're going to have to help me here, Lola. I can't do this by myself." I managed to get the thermal suit up over her body, her arms more or less into the sleeves, though she was limp as a rag doll and much heavier.

Her hand shot out and rested against my chest, stopping me. I looked up to see her eyes wide, nostrils flared, lips parted. She was staring down the corridor. I followed her gaze to see only shadows. Moving shadows.

I heard the sound of rending steel. Whatever had attacked Lola was still on board the outpost, and it was coming for us. I drew the flare gun from my pocket and loaded it. My hands shook, but the cartridges were huge and hard to miss.

The lights flickered. I placed the flare gun in Lola's lap and drew my legs into my thermal suit, cramming my feet into the boots and shoving my arms into the sleeves. I zipped up the torso and drew on the helmet. I didn't take the time to secure the seams or lace the boots. There was no time.

I kept glancing at the shadows at the end of the corridor, near the living quarters. As I bent to zip Lola's suit, I realized she was whispering something. And then she was screaming it.

Wendigo.

The command center behind me went dark, but I didn't turn to look. I clutched the flare gun, barely able to feel it through my gloves, and sidled toward the airlock. I punched a button and the airlock door slid open. "Lola! Go!" I shouted, aiming the flare gun at the roiling shadows, prepared to fire and bail.

The creature that stepped into the corridor was lit only by the emergency lights. In the soft yellow glow, it stood at least two meters tall, but it was so skinny I could make out its ribs. Its face had once been human, but it was now elongated, more like that of a wolf, with huge fangs bursting from its mouth. Its arms were long and grotesque, fingers tipped with deadly curved claws. Dark hair clung to its body in uneven patches, and between its legs there dangled a shriveled member that suggested it may once have been a man. It brought with it the reek of rotten meat and death.

It lunged for me, its mouth twisted in what might have been a grimace or a smile.

I fired the flare just as Lola lurched to her feet and shoved me into the airlock. The door slid shut with a hiss, separating me from her.

"Lola!" I screamed, pounding my fist against the door entry. It required a key code, and in my thermal suit my fingers were too bulky to enter the code. I shoved the flare gun into my pocket and started to pull off my right glove.

Lola appeared in the window. She was pale, but her eyes were fierce, burning in the orange light of the flare. She mouthed words. "I don't understand!" I yelled.

She mouthed the words again. This time I could make them out: "Heart of ice."

And then she was gone.

The creature appeared in the window. Up close, I could see that it was neither grimacing nor smiling, but that it had, instead, eaten away its own lips, lips now darkened with Lola's blood.

I scrambled for the outer door and onto the surface of Inyan. The wind howled like the souls of the damned, tugging at me with the force of a hurricane. I paused in the doorway, looking back, wondering whether the creature could follow me into the icy wind without a thermal suit. How could it? Nothing could survive such extreme temperatures. Nothing…human.

Wendigo. I thought about my grandfather and the stories of The People, stories I'd resented because they couldn't be mine, not with my blond hair and blue eyes, not without a Lakota name to give me legitimacy. The word was familiar and brought to mind a monster that had once been a man, a creature corrupted by tasting the blood of other men until all that remained was a ravenous husk fueled by a cold need, an empty yearning, a hunger. A creature with, legends said, a heart of ice.

The door shook, and a dent appeared from the inside. I jumped back; the wendigo had somehow managed to breach the airlock. I wasn't sure whether it could get through the reinforced steel door, but I didn't want to stick around and find out. Flicking on my headlamp, I turned and ran for the garage. Sweat blinded me and I tasted salt on my lips, salt and something else: Lola's blood running from my cheeks into my mouth. I gagged, stumbling, struggling to get back up, the thermal suit cumbersome.

I imagined that, behind me, I could hear steel bending and twisting beneath the screaming wind, and the sound pushed me forward.

I staggered to the garage and heaved open the door. The rover was parked just inside. I climbed on board and put the flare gun on the seat beside me—what should have been Lola's seat—and felt relief flood my aching limbs. Surely the rover could outrun a man, even one that had become a monster, especially one exposed to the frostbite-inducing cold of the moon's surface.

I brought up the display on my helmet with a flick of my eyes. "Daniel Teegan to *Thunderbird*. SOS."

"*Thunderbird* here."

I guffawed with joy. "Iron Cloud? Oh man, you have no idea how good it is to hear your voice!"

"Why the SOS? What's happening?"

"I need immediate evacuation. I'll be at the rendezvous ASAP."

"What about Lola?"

"No Lola. She...didn't make it." I swallowed hard against the lump that had risen in my throat. "Teegan out."

"Wait, what's happening? You can't just tell me Lola's..."

"Just meet me at the rendezvous! Teegan out!" Another flick of my eyes disabled the radio. I bit back tears. I couldn't afford to think about Lola right now. I couldn't let her sacrifice be for nothing.

I turned the key in the ignition and the rover's engine roared to life. The headlights illuminated a twisted silhouette in the garage doorway, blocking my path. Shuddering, I lowered my head, pressed the throttle to the floor, and then released the brake. The rover surged forward, snapping my head back, and charged toward the monster.

I was counting on the rover to make mincemeat of the wendigo. Instead, the creature crouched and affected a leap that would have been the envy of every professional lacrosse player in the Sioux Nation. I watched in the rearview as it landed nimbly behind the rover, dwindling as the vehicle carried me away.

I gunned the rover to its maximum speed, grateful for the smooth ground that offered no obstacles. The GPS in my helmet overlaid my path with a map, guiding me to the rendezvous coordinates.

Something heavy landed on the roof of the rover with a horrible *crunch*. The wendigo's upside-down face appeared in the windshield. I slammed on the brakes, expecting the wendigo's inertia to carry it forward as the rover stopped. But I underestimated the monster's strength. It held on, dropping down onto the hood to stare at me through the glass.

The wendigo punched the windshield, and though the glass was industrial space-grade, stars appeared. I screamed and reached for my only weapon, the flare gun on the passenger seat.

A second punch made larger cracks appear, less like stars and more like leggy spiders. Now cursing with fear, certain that my death was imminent—only a quarter klick from the rendezvous, my GPS assured me—I fumbled with the flare gun. My fingers in the suit were too bulky to operate the gun, and the remaining flares were in the pocket of my coveralls.

Panting, I put the flare gun in my left hand and

pushed off my right glove. I pulled my right hand into the thermal suit to dig in my coveralls for the flares.

The wendigo's third punch cracked the windshield so completely the monster was obscured from view. One more punch and he would be through. I maneuvered around the flare gun to open the door with my left hand and rolled out of the rover onto the frozen ground.

I pulled myself up and ran. I knew the wendigo followed me though I couldn't hear its footfalls over the wind. I found a flare in my pocket with my right hand and then shoved the hand back through the thermal suit's sleeve.

Timing would be everything. My hand would survive only a few seconds in the bitter cold. I would have to load the gun and fire it before frostbite set in.

And I would have to trust that Lola was right about the wendigo's heart of ice.

I jammed the flare into the gun and turned. The thermal suit was voluminous, not designed for sudden movement; my legs became tangled and I fell onto my back. The wendigo loomed above me. My hand was already starting to ache from the cold. I raised the flare gun and squeezed the trigger.

The flare struck the wendigo's chest and buried itself in the monster's ribs. A bright red light glowed from behind its flesh. It roared, a sound equal parts animal howl and human scream, staggering back from me to claw at its chest.

I scrambled to my feet and watched as the wendigo thrashed and groaned, dying in convulsions.

I drew my right arm back into the thermal suit, my fingers burning. I waited until the wendigo stopped thrashing. A few moments later, the flare in its chest sputtered out. In the distance, I could see the lights on the *Thunderbird* winking and flashing.

When I arrived at the rendezvous and the crew came out to meet me, they found me dragging the wendigo's corpse with my one good hand. They bundled me onto one stretcher and the wendigo onto another. We were wheeled into separate bays. Medical personnel stripped away my thermal suit and then I felt a quick pinch at my neck. A warm, languorous feeling spread through my body and my concerns about the wendigo became fuzzy.

I don't remember much after that until a few days later, when Paul Iron Cloud entered the medical bay. He glowered, dark eyes smoldering beneath heavy black brows.

"Did you even try to save her?"

"Nice to see you too, Iron Cloud," I said from the bed. My voice was raspy after days without use. I waved at him with the handless stump that capped my right arm.

"Answer the question."

"What do you think?" His accusation should probably have made me feel sad, or annoyed, or anything, but I just felt numb. He smelled strange, like a fresh steak, and my stomach churned.

"I think you left her to die." There were tears in his eyes. His mouth was a tight pucker.

I returned his glare with equal force. We'd never gotten along, because two men who love the same woman never do. He'd blame me for Lola's death no matter what I said. "Think what you like."

"Native Mining wants to celebrate you as a hero, you know. They're planning a Naming Ceremony and everything." Paul's eyes bored into me.

"I don't want a name," I growled.

"The crew families insist on it. Well, except Moon Walker's."

I flinched. Adam Moon Walker had been the astrophysicist aboard White Buffalo Outpost. The wendigo's DNA was a match for his. The nurses who gossiped over my bed whispered that he'd failed the psychological tests for living in the outpost's isolated conditions, but he'd been sent anyway. Whether a mere clerical error or malicious incompetence was responsible, nobody knew. The rest of the crew had been found in the mine shaft. They'd been trying to hide from the creature that had once been Moon Walker, presumably, and all that remained of them were clean-picked bones surrounded by the shredded remains of their thermal suits. Their families had sued Native Mining over the failed psychological tests and now, according to the nurses, they got whatever they wanted. Which, I guess, included canonizing me.

"I don't want a name," I repeated.

"Oh come on now, Teegan," Paul sneered, "we all know how much you want a name. You've whined about it your entire life. Poor little white boy, with his blond hair and blue eyes, never really Lakota. No matter what they name you, some of us will know you're not really one of The People. How could you be when you let Lola die?"

He stormed out, the dramatic effect of his exit somewhat lessened by the soft hiss of the door closing behind him. I retched over the railing of my bed onto the floor, my stomach once again rejecting the freeze-dried food, an action which summoned several nurses to swarm my bed.

A few hours later, Chief Red Star appeared at my bedside. "Choosing a name for you is proving difficult," he told me. "The families can't agree."

"I don't want a name." I gritted my teeth so hard they made a scraping sound. The noise reminded me of the wendigo rending the outpost's steel doors and a shudder shook my whole body.

Red Star patted my hand. He smelled salty and smoky, like beef jerky. "It's time, son. You've waited so long for this. You've earned the honor, and you wouldn't turn away a kind gesture by the families of those you avenged, would you? So tell me what you think: Daniel White Buffalo? Wendigo Slayer? Personally I like Blue Eyes, myself, though it doesn't reference your heroism…"

I stared at the knitting stump of my hand and thought of Lola's last words. My name had been an albatross around my neck my entire life, but maybe now it could be a reminder. A reminder of failure. A reminder of sacrifice.

"Iceheart," I said in a tone that allowed for no compromise, no argument.

Red Star blinked at me. "Daniel Iceheart. Has a nice ring to it."

"No," I said, flexing the nonexistent fingers of my amputated hand. "Just Iceheart."

The Chief nodded, sorrow flickering across his face. "I'll tell the families."

He got up and lumbered toward the door. I lay there, staring down at my wrist. The doctors would offer me a prosthetic, and I already knew I would refuse it. How could I walk around pretending I was whole when Lola was dead?

"See you for the Naming Ceremony tomorrow, Mister Teegan."

"Iceheart," I corrected him.

He hesitated in the doorway. "Lola Spotted Tail's death was the fault of the wendigo, you know," he said. "You can't blame yourself."

"Of course I can," I snarled. "She died on my watch, under my command. She was my responsibility."

He bowed his head. "The wendigo had a heart of ice, not you. No matter what your name." I let him have the last word as the door hissed shut behind him.

In my chest, my heart felt cold and hard, like a frozen stone. I remembered the taste of Lola's blood on my lips and shivered.

Invincible

Anyone who has been in combat will tell you that the bonds forged between soldiers are impenetrable. No other relationship can touch it. Out of all my soldiers, out of all the men and women whom I trusted and who trusted me, Ward was the one who fought at my side the longest. He was the bravest man I ever knew.

I just want you to understand why I didn't hesitate when the hospital called and told me he'd been found. If it had been Jamal or Demetrius or Michael, or any of the other dozens of men I've fought with over the years, I might have paused. But when the nurse told me James Ward was lying comatose in a hospital bed, my heart felt like it was going to explode. I hung up the phone and sobbed with joy. I hadn't let myself cry at all when Ward was declared missing and presumed dead. I'm the leader; I can't show weakness. All those emotions had been bottled up inside me and they just exploded outwards.

I made Michael drive me to the hospital in the van, because I didn't trust myself to take my bike, blubbering like I was. Visiting hours were nearly over but the nurse let us in. Some people don't recognize me without the leather mask, but others are more perceptive. I could tell from the way the nurse studied my face, pressed her lips into a thin line, and gestured wordlessly for me to follow her that she knew my identity.

She brought us to Ward's room. "Thank you," I told her.

The nurse nodded. "You saved my son Daniel once, about two years ago."

I smiled. "How's he doing?"

She shook her head, meeting my gaze with a sorrowful look. "He didn't leave the Crips, and got gunned down in a drive by."

"I'm so sorry." I meant it. The Crips had finally been whittled down to a manageable few core members, but it had taken years of steady undermining. I hated that so many lives had been lost in the meantime.

"No. Don't be sorry. He made his choices. Some people--some people just won't allow themselves to be saved." She never broke eye contact with me the whole time, as if she were afraid that if she blinked I would disappear. "I'll give you until 9:30, but then you gotta go. And keep it down, or the doctors might notice."

I nodded and retreated into the room, letting the nurse shut the door behind me. On the bed, lying on his back, was a figure I knew all too well. Ward's eyes were closed and his hands were pressed against his sides. His skin looked a shade darker than I remembered against the white bed sheets.

Michael sat in the chair on the other side of the room, his expression wary, watching Ward's face. "It sure as Hell looks like him."

I lifted the patient's left arm, the one nearest me, and studied it. His brown flesh was crisscrossed with scars, some fairly fresh and others older, from all the battles we'd fought together. I knew every scar by heart. "It looks like him 'cause it is him." I held up the arm. "See that long scar? Got that fighting the Brotherhood... March of last year? Yeah."

"I can't believe he's alive."

"I can. Ward's a tough piece of meat. Old man Death probably couldn't swallow him, and spit him back out so life can chew on him some more." Elated, I couldn't stop grinning.

"No, Kiara, I mean--that explosion. Nobody could have survived that. He shoulda been vaporized."

"But clearly he wasn't. He must've been thrown by the blast or something. Look at him. It's definitely Ward."

"Where's he been all this time?"

"The nurse said he turned up in an alley. Cops called the paramedics."

"It's been like a month. He can't have been passed out in an alley the whole time. Something's not right here."

Michael hadn't been on my team long, just a few months. I didn't have much respect for his opinion. "Hey, my second-in-command and best friend is alive. Can you just let me be happy for a minute?"

Michael scowled and looked away, crossing his arms over his chest.

"Kiara?" Ward's eyes blinked up at me.

"Oh! Sweet Jesus, he's awake!" I screamed.

"Shhhh! We're supposed to keep it down," Michael reminded me.

I covered my mouth but I couldn't stop laughing and shrieking. I threw my arms around Ward's barrel chest and breathed the cinnamon-nutmeg scent of his skin. And for the first time in a month, I felt like everything was going to be okay.

I could never have known how wrong I was.

Ward came home from the hospital a few days later--he had no health insurance and was, frankly, too stubborn to stay bedridden for long anyway. Jamal brought him home to the warehouse, where we threw a rather impromptu welcome-home party. He smiled, and thanked us, and tried to be jovial, but he was obviously exhausted. I sent him to bed.

In the middle of the night, I couldn't sleep, and crept to the men's barracks to peek at him. His feet hung over the end of the cot just as they always had. He snored softly. I wanted to crawl into bed with him and fall asleep to the sound of his breathing, like a little girl with her father, but I went back to my own bed instead.

My philosophy was to lead by example, so I always got up earlier than the rest of the troops and tried to put on a cheerful face, no matter how hard we'd worked or partied the night before. That morning, however, I came down the stairs onto the training floor to find Ward sitting on one of the benches. He was just staring across the room at nothing, his face slack.

"Ward?" I touched his arm.

"Kiara!" His eyes were the same chocolate-brown I remembered, but they were distant now. Like he was looking through me instead of at me. He smiled. "Good morning."

"Morning. You okay? You're up awful early."

He shrugged. "Couldn't sleep anymore. I made coffee." He gestured to the pot on the table in the corner.

"Thanks." I appreciated the gesture, but getting up early and brewing a pot was my job. My routine was interrupted and I didn't like it. I poured myself a mug anyway and tried to be gracious. "You want some?"

"Nah. Had some already."

We sat in silence for a few minutes while I sipped. "You look tired," I observed. "Maybe you should go back to bed."

"Bed's boring."

"You need rest to recover."

"I am recovered. I don't need to waste anymore time horizontal."

I hesitated, then asked: "Do you remember anything after the explosion?"

"What explosion?"

"The one we thought killed you. At the White Dragon meth lab."

Ward shook his head. "Nah, don't remember much of anything."

"So you don't know how you got in that alleyway."

"Nope. Why the interrogation, boss-lady?"

My old nickname made me smile. No one had called me that in a month. "Nothing just...hoping to figure out how you survived, who took care of you."

"Does it matter? I'm here now."

"I guess you're right, it doesn't matter."

He stood and shuffled to the door.

"Where you going?" I asked.

"Bathroom. I'm an old man, you know. Can't hold it like I used to." We both chuckled, because he was only 42 years old, but had lived longer than anyone involved in vigilante justice had a right to. He'd certainly outlived most of his former buddies in the Crips.

The rest of the gang appeared, lured by the scent of coffee into the training area. I put us all to work sparring with crowbars and pipes. Ward insisted on participating, but his reactions were slow. I made him sit out and use the stopwatch to time the matches.

After sparring, we split up to do our daily business. It was only then that I realized all of Ward's daily tasks had been reassigned after his disappearance. He had nothing to do.

"Why don't you go take a nap," I suggested.

"I'm not that old. And you've apparently forgotten how tough I am. I'm the same man who took six bullets for your army, remember? Stop treating me like I'm made of glass." He balled his huge hands into fists.

"I have nothing for you to do and you need to rest anyway," I insisted.

"He can come on the recon mission with me," Jamal volunteered. His assignment for the day was to stalk the new player in town.

So Jamal took Ward for a few hours, leaving me in peace to do my paperwork. That's what they don't tell you about running a vigilante crime-fighting organization--there's paperwork. Lots of it. More than you would expect, anyway.

I was listening to the radio and filling out a form for the LAPD about our latest arrests when Ward stormed into my office. "Kiara..."

I stood. "What's up?"

"The pictures we got..."

Jamal followed him at a more sedate pace. "Ward thinks he recognizes the guy." He handed me the digital camera so I could take a look.

The pictures were of a middle-aged white guy. He was pretty nondescript except for a receding hairline. "This it?"

"You don't recognize him?" Ward demanded.

"No. Should I?"

"Remember that email we got a few months ago, about Captain Hero? It had an attachment."

I remembered that email all too vividly. Captain Hero was every super-powered vigilante's role model. He was supposed to be indestructible, but someone had taken him down. The email had been a warning to look out for that someone.

They called him The Mercenary.

I sat down at the laptop and found the file. "It could be him," I said, using the zoom feature on the camera to get a better look at the images. "He's so tiny in these pictures it's hard to tell."

"Sorry, that's the closest we could get without giving away our position," Jamal said.

"Why would the Mercenary be in LA making waves anyway?" I asked.

"Don't you get it?" Ward's voice was deep, but now it carried a shrill edge of panic I'd never heard before. "He's here to kill you, Kiara. Panthera is his next victim."

Jamal and I stared in silence. It made too much sense to be false. The gangs and crime families of LA had wanted me dead for years. Who better to do it than the man who took out Captain Hero?

"Did you find his hideout?" I asked Jamal.

"He's staying in the Ritz Carlton on Olympic."

"Wait, what? He's staying in a hotel?"

"Under the name Travis Johnson. Ward here talked a desk clerk into giving up his room number, too. Room 517."

Ward chuckled. "Travis Johnson. Whitest name I've ever heard."

"Good work...both of you. Let's saddle up the cavalry."

"Shouldn't we come up with a plan first?" Ward asked.

"No time. We need to bring the fight to him, before he can bring it to us. The best defense..."

"Is a good offense," Both men intoned. It was a phrase I used way too much, but it had proven to be true countless times.

While they gathered our manpower, I got dressed. In his biography, Captain Hero talks extensively about the drama of a good costume, something original, memorable, and iconic. Something that will make criminals think twice before crossing you, and give innocents a rallying symbol. I think he goes on about it a bit long, truth be told, and the outfit is less important than the crime-fighting itself...but I digress. My costume was all black leather. It was comfortable for riding my bike to crime scenes, and it looked badass. I'd say it also gave me an extra layer of protection that other fabrics don't, but the truth is that with my super powers, I didn't really need an extra layer of protection.

I pressed the Panthera mask against my face last of all. It was held in place with a layer of spirit gum. It would sting a little when I peeled it off later, but it was totally worth it. I can't pretend that it gave me anonymity; a lot of folks recognized me without it. But I wore it anyway, because it was a uniform. Panthera was more than a costume, more than a name. She was a persona, an aspect of myself. I felt ten feet tall wearing that mask.

Ward, Jamal, and the others had gathered on the warehouse floor. There were ten people in my army back then, eight men and two women. Eleven counting Ward. Some of them wore Kevlar; others couldn't be bothered. They each carried their favorite weapon. I joined them, my leather outfit creaking. "Your objective is to cut off the exits and try to capture the Mercenary, aka Travis Johnson. Has everyone seen his picture?" Nods. "Good. Don't let him get away. It could be the difference between life and death for our little operation here. I'll meet you at the Ritz Carlton."

This was a strategy we'd used a hundred times before: I stormed in the front door, while my people cut off the exits. If I had speed, like Captain Hero, I wouldn't need help, but my only superpower was my chitinous shell. It granted me invulnerability and strength, but not quickness. Before I recruited and put together a team, dozens of gangbangers escaped me by just running away. I'm only five-foot-seven, and the chitinous shell makes me heavier than a normal woman my size, so I'm not going to be winning any footraces.

But I didn't need to be fast with an army at my side.

Driving my bike through the streets of LA was always a combination of thrilling and harrowing. I wouldn't be a very good superhero if I didn't get a thrill out of danger, but neither do I have a death wish, so I keep the stunts to a minimum. It was morning, not my usual time for being out and about, but people still stared and pointed and smiled, recognizing me. I wondered how many black-clad women on Suzuki GS500E motorcycles were mistaken for Panthera.

I arrived at the hotel and parked my bike in the underground parking garage. The attendants recognized me and when I removed my helmet, they asked for photos. I made them promise to wait several hours before selling or uploading the photos onto the internet, but that's not a promise a lot of people can keep. I figured The Mercenary probably knew I was coming anyway. He'd be prepared, regardless of whether the parking attendants gave away my location.

I called Jamal from the elevator. "You in position?"

"Give us a few minutes. You're too fast on that bike."

"Yeah, yeah. I'll take my time and get my bearings. I suspect we're only dealing with one guy though. Shouldn't be too complicated."

The fifth floor of the Ritz Carlton looked just like the fifth floor of any hotel, only fancier. The walls were covered in burgundy wallpaper with a pattern of tiny gold diamonds, and the floors were carpeted with crazy spirals and whorls in many colors. A maid's cart was sitting in the hall but no maid was apparent. I found my way to room 517 and paused, waiting for Jamal's go-ahead.

The door to room 517 swung open. The middle-aged white man from Jamal's photos was standing there, smiling as if I were an old friend he'd been expecting.

"Miss Bell? Do come in."

His voice made me shudder involuntarily. There was something so cold, so calculating, so casual about it. This man was here to kill me, and he was smiling like we were pals. He knew my real name, and used it without malice. This was my death, the most personal thing in the world to me, but to him, it was all business. How do you reason with someone like that? I started to sweat under my leathers.

"Mr. Johnson." I stepped into the hotel room.

I've been in a few hotel rooms in my life, but nothing like this Ritz Carlton suite. The man had his own kitchen. Vaulted ceilings. Giant windows swathed in velvet curtains. It was all I could do to keep my mouth from gaping open and keep my wits about me.

The door clicked shut behind me. My host shuffled past me into the part of the suite set up like my grandmother's parlor, all sofas and wingback chairs around a fireplace that probably produced actual flames. "Please have a seat," he offered, gesturing to a chair and seating himself.

"No thank you, I'll stand."

He sighed. "Well, alright then. I probably would too, in your situation. It won't help you though."

"What would?"

Now he smirked. "I suppose if you could buy the contract on your life, that might deter me."

"How much?"

"Four million dollars."

I swallowed hard. "I don't have that kind of cash. I'm a vigilante superhero. I can barely keep the lights on and feed my people with donations."

He waved his hand. "I'm aware of your finances. Four million is an impressive sum, by the way. Almost as much as I got killing Captain Hero." He rose and walked to a table with bottles of liquids in shades of amber and brown. "Would you care for a drink?"

My cheeks burned with rage. This man killed Captain Hero, my role model, and now he was casually discussing his price and offering me a drink? "Can we just get on with this?"

The Mercenary didn't immediately reply. He took his time pouring a drink and swishing it in the glass. He sipped and nodded. "Get on with what?"

"You're going to try to kill me, and I'm going to take you apart."

His laugh was unexpectedly high and even more unnerving than his speaking voice. "Try to kill you? Oh no, no, no, no."

"Isn't that why you're here? You're an assassin for hire."

"Well, yes, in a manner of speaking. But my assignment isn't so much to kill you as to incapacitate you. The gentlemen who hired me don't care what happens to you, just as long as you leave them alone and let them go about their business. And the fact is, you're right: if I tried to kill you by conventional means, you undoubtedly would take me apart."

"Then what's your game?" My heart felt like a

cold, hard lump behind my ribs.

He smirked again, and this time when he raised his eyes to me over the rim of his glass there was a twinkle of malice there. "You'll see soon enough. Finding your weakness though--that was a challenge. One I probably would have undertaken for half the price, though I'd appreciate it if you didn't reveal that to anyone. I do love a good puzzle."

I almost couldn't bring myself to ask, but I had to know. "What's my weakness then?"

"Well, let's see. Your chitinous shell makes you invulnerable from traditional weapons, even fire. It also allows you to be inhumanly strong. So in a fair fight against you, anyone would lose--maybe even Captain Hero. You're not very fast, I expect because the shell, even when it's not activated on a cellular level, weighs you down, but you've overcome that little problem, haven't you? You recruited other people to help you. Other people you care about. Friends."

"Family," I corrected him.

His smile broadened. "Precisely."

I started to make a witty retort, but just at that moment The Mercenary's face started to melt. The corners of his mouth drooped, his chin elongated, his fingers sagged toward the floor. His eyes burned like hot coals. I took a step back from him and fumbled for the doorknob.

"What are you?" I gasped.

"Ah, about time," he said, and though he continued talking, the rest of his words were lost. He was right before me, with his twisting mouth, but his voice sounded like it was coming to me from the other side of a wall made of mattresses.

I ran into the hallway, letting the door slam behind me, and pulled my phone from my pocket. I speed-dialed Jamal.

"Kiara?" His voice was distant, as if he were shouting into the phone from down a long corridor.

"He's not human," I cried into the phone. "The Mercenary isn't a man at all, he's a demon. A horrible thing. We have to get away."

"Kiara, I can't understand you." His voice was so tiny.

"WE HAVE TO RUN!" I screamed. I dropped the phone and ran.

I don't really remember what happened next all that clearly. The hotel transformed into a lake of fire, the walls full of eyes that watched me. Hands grabbed for me. Sinister voices called my name. Creatures out of nightmare lunged for me.

One of them had Ward's voice. "Kiara, I'm so sorry," he cried, even as he transformed into a dragon made of jagged glass. I called my chitinous shell, hardening only my hands, and punched him until he stopped saying my name.

I regained consciousness in a small white room. It looked like a hospital room, but there were no windows. The lights seemed far too bright. An IV was sticking out of my arm. I really hate IVs, there's something awful about a piece of metal or plastic inserted into your body where it's not supposed to be. When I moved to rip the thing out, I found that my wrists were bound to the bed rails with velcro straps.

I called my chitinous shell, intending to explode the straps, but it didn't respond. I tried again and again to summon it, until I was weeping with effort. Finally I collapsed and lay staring up at the ceiling. Someone had taped a poster above the bed, a poster of a kitten clinging to a branch. "Hang in there," the poster advised.

The door opened and a nurse entered. When she saw I was awake she gasped and then smiled. "I'll get Doctor Lund for you honey, you just stick around, okay?"

She didn't give me time to respond.

Moments later the door opened and a tall, pale man walked in. He wore a nicely tailored suit complete with a tie-tack and everything. I couldn't see his shoes but I would have been willing to bet they were those expensive square-toed Italian ones. He dragged a stool to my bedside and smiled at me.

"Miss Bell, I'm Doctor Erasmus Lund." He had a subtle, lilting accent I couldn't place.

"Where am I?" I tried to say, but the words came out as a rasping cough.

The nurse brought me water and Doctor Lund held the glass so I could drink through a straw. My mouth wet, I asked the question a second time.

"You're at my medical resort on an island in the Atlantic Ocean," he told me. He placed the glass on the bedside table and unstrapped my hands. "How much do you remember?"

I shook my head. "Remember about what?"

"The Mercenary. You went to meet him at a hotel."

I reeled as the memories came crashing back, but they were a jumble. "He was...wrong. I thought he was a monster. I ran." My wrists itched from long confinement in the straps and I rubbed at them. "How did I get here? What happened?"

Doctor Lund seated himself again. "We rescued you from a mental institution for the criminally insane." One of his pale hands rested on mine and squeezed gently. "You're among friends now."

"A mental institution? I'm not insane."

He nodded. "You aren't now. But the Mercenary used a potent cocktail of drugs...you were hallucinating for almost three weeks."

"Hallucinating?" I repeated dumbly.

Doctor Lund patted my hand. "The effects have worn off now, as we knew they would if we waited and kept you hydrated."

"My team. Where's my team? Where's Ward? And Jamal?" I knew the answer. I remembered driving my fists into the face of a monster with Jamal's amber eyes, of beating to death a creature with Ward's pleading cries. My lungs felt tight, constricted, as if they were going to be crushed under the weight of my sorrow.

"Perhaps we should talk about that another day. You need to rest. I'll give you a sedative for now." He gestured to the nurse.

I grabbed his hand, and that made me realize that something wasn't quite right with my own hand. My shell was partially activated. Half my hand was paralyzed because it was encased. I tried to make the shell contract, but it wouldn't obey. "Tell me what happened," I demanded. "How did he break me?"

"The drugs he administered were a unique blend of hallucinogens and others…others we've never even seen before. We're trying to undo the damage but it's going to take time. The drugs damaged your DNA somehow so your shell is no longer in your control."

I'd had my shell to protect me my entire life. I felt naked and vulnerable without it. "What about my friends? Ward? Jamal?"

Doctor Lund sighed. "I'm sorry to say they're all dead."

"I--I killed them, didn't I?" I had already worked out the answer, but I had to hear it.

"Yes. But you didn't know what you were doing. It's not your fault."

"How. How did he get the drugs in me?" I could barely ask the question. I suspected I knew the answer to this one, too.

"One of your team members must have snuck it into your food."

"Coffee," I corrected him. "Coffee."

He nodded. "That would do it, yes. You should rest before we talk about this more. Your first priority is to regain your strength." He rose and the nurse came over to inject something into my IV. "Doctor's orders."

"Can you fix me?" I stared at his face, looking for clues.

He smiled down at me. "It will take time and hard work, but yes. I think we can."

The sedative took effect and I leaned back against the pillows. My grief was now light as a feather, hovering somewhere above me. "Why?"

"Why what? Why will we fix you?" He chuckled. "That's what we do here."

"No. Why...the Mercenary...my friends..." Tears escaped my eyes and trickled down my cheeks to drip into my ears.

Doctor Lund leaned over me and squeezed my hand. His eyes were the iciest blue I've ever seen. "Because he had no other way to hurt you, I'm afraid. You're invincible."

Long Time, No See

Ayida's eyes were blank. She was only a child the first time I met her, still unfinished, but even so, I saw the space where a soul should be. My skin prickled when she looked at me with her vacant face.

"Your daughter will become a powerful *mambo*," I told her mother in the marketplace. "You should let me take her for training right away."

"How can you know such a thing?"

"I can see it when I look at her. I can read the bones," I offered, reaching for the pouch at my side. "The *loa* can prove my words."

"That's silly superstitious nonsense."

Bile-flavored rage bubbled up in my throat. "I've built my life around such silly superstitious nonsense." I bit back further angry words. "Let me show you, please. The *hounfour* is right around the corner. It will only take a few moments and it could change your daughter's life." Still she hesitated, so I pressed on. "My name is Erzulie Tio, and I've been reading the bones since I was not much older than your girl."

"Erzulie Tio? I've heard of you."

Of course she'd heard of me. "From your

neighbors?"

"Yes. They said you freed their son from a demon."

"Not a demon, a Petwo *loa*. But yes, I coaxed the spirit from the boy. Let me read the bones for your daughter. You're part of our community now, so your spiritual welfare falls to me."

She licked her lips, conflicting beliefs warring on her face.

"Mama, please?" The girl turned those big, empty pools up to her mother and the woman at last smiled and nodded.

"Yes, alright."

I brought them to the *hounfour* and cleared a circle on the dirt floor, squatting beside it. "What's your name, child?"

"Ayida Fazande," she replied, kneeling and watching my hands with intense interest. I drew the bones from their pouch and she asked, "Are they real bones?"

"*Yapok* knuckles." I held out my palm studded with bones. Each knuckle was marked with mystical symbols.

"They look like dice." The girl's mother inspected the bones too, leaning down over her child. They looked so much alike, mother and daughter, nearly identical, Ayida the smaller and less scarred version.

One soul can't inhabit two bodies.

"Please stand back, Mrs. Fazande."

She smiled and took a step back, saying, "Call me Lourdes."

I muttered a quick prayer to Papa Legba and threw the bones into the circle. They scattered and rolled, like they always do. I prepared to announce the fate I'd already determined for Ayida, but my breath hitched in my throat as the scattered knuckles told me a story. A story of power. A story of blood. A story of the terrible things that lurk in the darkness. Shrill screams made my ears ache and my nose burned with the stench of searing flesh. And through it all there was Ayida Fazande, flames dancing in her eyes.

"Erzulie? Erzulie are you alright?" Lourdes Fazande stood over me. "Should we get the doctor?"

I was prone on the floor, and the fire was gone. "No, no, I'll be fine," I assured her, sitting up. I scanned the room for Ayida. The girl was standing in the doorway, her empty eyes wide with fear and staring at me.

"What happened?" Lourdes asked, offering her hand to help me climb to my feet.

"The *loa* spoke," I replied, still watching Ayida.

"What did they say?"

"Your daughter has power. She is destined for..." I shook my head, conflicted. "...greatness. I should begin her *mambo* training immediately."

"*Mambo* training? If she's destined for greatness then she can do better than this." Lourdes's gesture swept over the *hounfour*. The mud-and-straw walls, the swept dirt floors, the glassless windows. Her gaze even included me, in my simple cotton dress, barefoot and childless. "I want more for Ayida than this life."

A matter of disappearing chickens brought me to the Fazande's doorstep not long after our first meeting. Neighbors had complained to me that their fowl were missing. I'd discovered the birds deep in the forest, following a trail of feathers and blood, thinking perhaps a wild dog was the culprit. Instead I found headless chicken corpses, a circle of blood, and dirt tamped down by dancing.

My feet carried me to the Fazande's house. Lourdes and Ayida were working in the garden with the rest of the family. When Lourdes spotted me she called for all the children to hide in the house.

"What are you doing here? We don't want to talk to you!" She brushed sweat from her forehead, leaving streaks of dirt, squinting against the bright sun.

"I found dead chickens in the forest," I blurted. "Someone has been stealing them from your neighbors and using them for...for vodou rites."

"What does that have to do with us?"

"I think it was Ayida."

Lourdes scoffed. "Ayida knows less than nothing about your vodou rites."

"Your daughter is special."

"I know. That's no reason for me to send her with you."

"You must." I looked up at movement on the porch. Ayida stood there, staring. I suppressed a shudder. "There's something...I didn't tell you."

Lourdes followed my gaze and shouted for Ayida to get back in the house. "This thing you didn't tell me, is it something that will convince me to send Ayida with you?"

"Yes. She's..."

"You should have told me before. Now I don't believe you. Now I think you're desperate."

"I am desperate. Your daughter..."

"No. I can't make it any clearer. You should go before Papa comes home."

"Your papa respects me. If you won't listen, he will."

"Papa also owns a gun. Are you willing to take the chance he'll side with you?"

My retort was interrupted by a warm, salty breeze and the distant rumble of thunder. Both Lourdes and I turned to the horizon, where dark clouds boiled. We nodded to one another, an unspoken agreement that our human concerns could wait in the face of the coming storm.

I hurried back to the village. My neighbors were boarding up their homes and shops. With the help of a few neighborhood boys, I just managed to get the windows of the *hounfour* shuttered before the rain arrived.

The word "rain" is barely sufficient to describe a summer storm in Haiti. Torrent is a better word. The world was silenced and stopped by the force of the winds and the huge, pelting droplets. Even the human smells that always surrounded us, odors of sweat and garbage and cooking and sex and birth and death, were obliterated by the clean, fresh scent of water.

Alone but for a few guttering candles, I used the time to sweep the floors and clean the walls with my special tonic. The room filled with the scents of pepper and herbs, backed by the cleanliness of vinegar, the scent of a room purified both physically and spiritually. I always found comfort in that scent, because it reminded me of the *mambo* who trained me, who taught me to brew the tonic from wine, and cast the bones, and pray to the *loa*. I could feel her beside me, singing as I worked, and I felt less afraid.

I prayed for a while, seeking guidance from the *loa*, but the guidance never came. Eventually exhaustion won out over my vigil and I curled up on my cot in the back of the *hounfour*. Lulled by the grumble of thunder and the tap of rain against the aluminum roof, I dozed.

Pressure against my throat startled me awake. Ayida's face loomed in my vision, her mouth twisted into a snarl. Her small hands were about my neck, strangling me. I shoved her back and sent her sprawling across the dirt floor.

"What are you doing?" I croaked, rising from the cot.

Ayida crouched on all fours like an animal. She bared her teeth and growled at me, snapping at the air. Her eyes were full of blind rage.

I fumbled for the bottle of tonic and the broom. Ayida lunged at me and I poked her in the belly with the broom, keeping her away from me, while I called for Papa Legba. "Take this *loa* from this child," I called, and splashed the tonic at the girl.

Ayida screamed and covered her face, crumpling to the floor. I dropped the broom and wrapped one arm around her, still clutching the tonic bottle in my other hand and calling for Papa Legba. "Call the *loa* back across the divide, Father of the Crossroads! Release this girl!" I sprinkled more tonic onto her hair, the scent of pepper and vinegar surrounding us like a caustic cloud. My eyes burned and I squeezed them shut.

Thunder exploded all around us and Ayida shrieked with fear, writhing in my grasp. I wish I could say that it was my tonic that drove the *loa* away, or perhaps the intervention of Papa Legba, but I have to give credit to Agau, the spirit of thunder. His voice rolled and clashed and encompassed us for a few moments, as if the house were in the center of the storm. His brutality was so frightening that the *loa* gripping her body fled and Ayida went limp in my arms when the thunder had passed.

I lowered the girl to my cot. She whimpered and curled into the fetal position, tears streaming down her face to leave silvery tracks across her dark skin.

"I'll get you some water." I rose, but her hand shot out and grasped my arm. "What is it, child?"

Her voice was small and distant when she spoke. "Can you make them stop?"

"Make who stop what?"

"The *loa*. Can you make them stop?"

My chest felt tight in sympathy. "With training and hard work, yes. Together, we can make them stop."

She released me and I went to find her water. She stayed the night in the *hounfour*, draped across my lap, and I sang her the songs of the *mambo* while I wiped the tonic from her face with a wet cloth.

The thunder gradually grew less and less fearsome until it stopped altogether, and not long after the rain stopped as well. The crickets and frogs returned to their chirping and buzzing. I threw open the shutters to greet a hot morning that was quickly becoming stifling.

Ayida was asleep on my cot and I was boiling plantains for breakfast when Lourdes Fazande appeared. She threw open the door, glanced about, issued a strangled cry of relief, and ran to her daughter. Behind her followed her father, an imposing farmer holding a gun, and two of the young men who worked on his farm.

I nodded greeting to the men. "You'll find the girl unharmed."

Kneeling by the cot, Lourdes checked her daughter for injuries. "Her face is swollen. What did you do?"

"A *loa* was riding her." I gestured to the now-empty bottle of tonic on the floor near the bed.

"Mama? Mama, Erzulie Tio hurt me." Ayida's voice sounded nasal and strange, but Lourdes didn't seem to notice.

"What did you do?" Lourdes demanded of me as she pulled her daughter to her feet and clutched the child to her side.

"I defended myself and saved her from the *loa*. Nothing more."

"She hurt me," Ayida insisted. She pushed away from her mother. "She touched me *here*." She cupped her nether regions.

Lourdes's mouth puckered in fury. "This ends now. If you touch my daughter again, I'll kill you. Do you understand?"

"She came to me. I didn't take her, and..."

"I don't care! If she comes to you again, if you so much as speak to her in the marketplace, I'll make you wish you'd never been born. Come, Ayida." She grabbed her daughter's hand and tugged her toward the door.

Ayida didn't move for a moment. Dark intelligence flickered in her eyes. Her lips curled in a sneer. "*A pi ta*, 'Zulie. See you on the other side."

The trek through the jungle was not an easy one. It required the better part of a day and a full pack of supplies. When I finally approached the clearing where an old man crouched over a fire pit, afternoon was preparing to give way to evening.

"Erzulie Tio! *Sa fè lon temps nou pa we!*" The man squatting by the fire stood and waved. His voice was the same booming bass I remembered from years gone by, though he was no longer the towering giant of a man he once was. Twenty years ago I had likened my friend to a wild boar, substantial and intimidating, but now he reminded me more of an ancient tree, with brown limbs so frail they looked like they might break in a strong wind.

"Manno Roche!" I called. "*Bonswa*, my friend." We met halfway between the path and the fire pit. We clasped hands, and Manno pulled me into his embrace.

I kissed his cheek and then, overwhelmed by emotion, I planted another kiss firmly on his mouth.

He laughed. "I'm happy to see you too, Erzulie." He turned to the house. "Sylvenie! Come quick, it's Erzulie Tio!"

Manno's wife emerged from the house. She had barely aged since our last encounter, still beautiful and shapely. She smiled reluctantly and waved from the porch but didn't approach.

"What brings you all the way out here?" Manno asked.

"Let me sit and have some water and I'll tell you."

We went to the porch and Sylvenie brought us a table, two small chairs, and a big pitcher of water. I drank and made small talk, asking about their life in the jungle, and then when I had recovered my breath, I told them about Ayida Fazande.

When I finished, Sylvenie disappeared silently into the house. Manno sat back in his chair and stared off into the distance for a few moments before speaking. "You're sure it was Baron Kriminel?"

"No one else calls me 'Zulie."

Manno stared at his own hands. "What do you want me to do?"

"I want to call Agau."

"Are you mad? I can't call Agau. Look at me, Erzulie. This body couldn't stand to be mounted by

Papa Legba. Agau is brutal. You're asking me to sacrifice myself."

"Then I'll do it. You do the ritual, and Agau can mount me instead."

Manno studied me closely. "These visions really have you spooked, to offer that."

"I'm desperate. And Agau frightened the *loa* once before...I believe he could do it again. Maybe permanently."

"You used to hate being ridden."

"I still hate it. Ever since..." I swallowed against the lump of fear in my throat.

"Ever since we tried to call Baron Samedi and got Kriminel instead."

I grimaced. "But I don't see what choice we have. The alternative is unthinkable."

Sylvenie brought us wooden bowls full of rice and beans. "I forbid either of you to make a decision on empty stomachs."

I accepted the food and watched as my friend's wife handed him a bowl and spoon and lovingly kissed his forehead before retreating into the house.

"She seems sad," I offered.

Manno frowned. "She is sad. She has always been sad, my Sylvenie. She has always known a day would come when someone would need the vodou, and it would be my undoing. She knows this will probably kill me."

"Not if I let the *loa* use my body."

"Even if you let the *loa* use your body, Erzulie. The cancer has taken its toll. There's not much left of me to give."

I had no reply to that, so I ate instead. We sat for a long time, watching twilight conquer the jungle, listening to the birds grow quiet and the insects grow louder. Eventually, our bellies full, we set the bowls aside and Manno sighed.

"Did you bring a chicken?"

"I can't ask for your life. If I had known..."

"Let my death be a sacrifice. Soon I'll be going to see Baron Samedi either way. It might as well be in service to a greater purpose."

"But Sylvenie..."

"Promise me you'll take her back to the village with you. Don't let her stay here when I'm gone."

Numb, I could only nod. "There's a chicken in my pack."

"And what about the girl?"

My gaze settled on the tree line. "She'll come. Baron Kriminel and I have unfinished business."

We built a massive bonfire in the fire pit. Manno sacrificed the chicken and smeared its blood on my forehead and chest. He sat beside the fire with a pair of drums and beat frantic music while Sylvenie and I danced. We pushed ourselves past the point of exhaustion, chanting and singing even when we were out of breath. Eventually, after hours of this, I felt myself step from my thrashing body, and I knew the time had come for Agau to mount me. The sacred trance had removed my doubt and fear, leaving me apathetic, vacant, ready to be ridden.

I felt Agau's spirit thrumming in my bones, his consciousness filling me until it felt like he would split my skin. But then, suddenly, I was empty, and my own soul snapped back into my body. I collapsed to the ground, disoriented. "Agau! Agau, come back!" My voice was hoarse with overuse.

Manno slid off his chair onto the ground and began to convulse. Sylvenie and I ran to his side and tried to protect him from hurting himself. His body became stiff and for a moment, I feared he was dead. But then he relaxed in our arms, and sat up.

He laughed, and it was a sound like rocks rubbing together, low and gruff. When he spoke his voice was even deeper and more resonant than usual. "*Bonswa*, my chickadees. I'm hungry."

Wiping tears from her cheeks, Sylvenie went to fetch food.

"You were supposed to take me," I told Agau. "Why didn't you take me?"

"I don't want to mount you. I want to *mount* you!" Manno's hands pressed the flesh of my thighs and his mouth went for my neck.

Desire surged through me at the feel of his callused fingers and hot breath on my neglected skin, but I pushed him away. "No! We're not here for that! We're here to talk about a girl. Ayida Fazande."

"Hungry." He reached for me.

"Sylvenie is bringing food."

"Not just for food, woman!" He pulled me to him roughly.

"First we talk about the girl." I pushed away and rose, stepping back from him.

"First we sate my needs." He stood as well, grabbing at me again. "I am the god of thunder. You called me here. Now you will do as I command."

He chased me around the fire, growling and grunting, until Sylvenie appeared with plates laden with food. He crouched over the plates and shoved handfuls of chicken and rice into his mouth, eating loudly and with no care for manners.

"We called you because we need you to protect Ayida Fazande," I said as he ate, careful to stay an arm's length away from him.

Manno's eyes—Agau's eyes—locked on mine. "And what will you give me in exchange? My protection comes with a price."

"I'll marry you. No *loa* has ever claimed me."

"Baron Kriminel says otherwise."

"Baron Kriminel is a liar."

He smiled. "That much is true. But I don't want you. You're too old." His glanced at Sylvenie.

She gasped. "I'm already married."

"I would claim you only once a week."

Sylvenie turned to me. "This was not part of the bargain."

"You can have her once a month and me as well," I offered.

"And the girl."

I shook my head. "I can't make that bargain. Ayida is too young. And her parents aren't here to bargain for her."

"All three or nothing at all." Agau tossed chicken bones into the fire.

"No bargain." Ayida appeared just outside the ring of light cast by the fire. She was filthy, her clothes caked with muck and body smeared with what might be blood or might be something else. Her voice was still high and nasal.

"Ayida!" I took a step toward her, and then stopped, catching myself. "Baron Kriminel."

"Aren't you clever." Kriminel stepped into the firelight, walking with a masculine swagger. Ayida's arms were riddled with bite marks—human bite marks—

probably from her own mouth.

"What have you done to her?"

Kriminel chortled. "What do you care? The girl is an empty vessel, waiting to be filled. No soul, or such a tiny one that it's inconsequential. She's barely more than an animal, and you sacrifice those to my kind regularly."

"She's a person, and you're hurting her."

Kriminel ignored me and instead turned to Agau. Manno stood, towering over the tiny girl even in his decrepit state. "Baron. I see you're still mounting children, like a pathetic weakling."

Ayida's body moved faster than any serpent I've ever seen. With a growl, she barreled into Manno and knocked him to the ground. Screaming, the two *loa* fought each other, punching and kicking and biting, abusing the human bodies they possessed.

"We have to stop them!" Sylvenie cried.

"Get more food!" I told her. She ran for the house.

I grabbed the bottle of tonic from my pack and doused the fighting *loa* with the liquid. They both screamed and reeled away from one another. "Stop this!" I shouted. "Agau, do you see now why I want protection for the girl? She's too easy for the lowest of spirits to mount."

Agau glared at me through red-rimmed eyes. "I don't care about the girl. I don't care about any of you!"

His voice boomed, startling birds in the jungle to take flight in a flurry of wings.

Baron Kriminel laughed, a sinister sound that made me shiver. "Your gambit to save the girl has failed. But I will offer you a bargain even if he won't."

Sylvenie appeared with bowls of food and laid them at the feet of the two *loa*. They both squatted and used their hands to scoop pork and plantains into their mouths. "What bargain do you offer?" I asked breathlessly, terrified of the answer.

"Marry me as you should have done twenty years ago."

The world was suddenly hazy, my vision a tunnel. "What would be the terms?"

"You'd be my wife. You'd do my bidding. You'd let me mount you whenever I choose. In exchange, I'll leave the girl alone."

Sylvenie moved beside me and laid a gentle hand on my arm. "You can't do this, Erzulie. To be married to Baron Kriminel would be the cruelest fate I can imagine."

I remembered the stink of burning flesh and the piercing screams of my vision. "There are crueler fates." I turned to Kriminel. "I'll marry you if you'll give the girl your protection. No *loa* are to mount her, ever, for the remainder of her life."

Kriminel stood, his mouth smeared with grease.

"You would make this bargain for her?"

"Not only for her."

"NO." Agau threw his bowl aside like a petulant toddler. "The women are mine. I will protect the girl! Not you, pathetic scum." He advanced on Kriminel.

I called for him to stop, but it was too late. This time Agau wasn't interested in a brawl. He laid his hands on Ayida's shoulders. His mouth opened and the sound that emerged was thunder, but louder than any thunder I'd ever heard, so loud it shook the ground. Ayida struggled for a moment, and then her eyes grew wide and her body went limp.

Agau gently laid her on the ground. "Baron Kriminel is no match for the god of thunder."

I hurried to Ayida and laid my hand on her chest to be sure she was still breathing. When her ribcage rose and fell I let out a laugh that was half relief and half disbelief. "Thank you," I breathed to Agau, hardly believing I'd so narrowly missed such a terrible future. Ayida was safe; we were all safe.

"Don't thank me yet," Agau replied. Manno's arms opened and he smiled lasciviously.

Sylvenie and I went to him without hesitation.

In the morning, Sylvenie and I awoke in Manno's arms. His mouth was curved in a beatific smile, but his body was stiff and cold. I covered Manno's still form with the blanket, my mind still hazy with memories of the night before, memories of skin and mouths and hot, wet darkness. Sylvenie smiled, though it was full of sorrow, and I couldn't help smiling myself.

Ayida was sitting on the porch.

"*Bonjou*, Ayida," I said quietly, cautiously.

"*Bonjou*, Erzulie Tio," she replied, turning to look at me. Gray clouds roiled behind her eyes, dark with the promise of rain.

I breathed a sigh of relief. "Let's go home."

Sylvenie took my hand. "You know that it's not over, don't you? You've deceived Baron Kriminel twice now. He'll come for you again, as soon as he has a chance."

I nodded, squeezing Sylvenie's fingers and reaching for Ayida's hand. "Agau saved me this time. Next time I probably won't be so lucky."

"Then why do you smile, Erzulie Tio?" Ayida asked, and I noticed that her voice sounded deeper and more resonant than it had before.

"Because you are safe, Ayida, and that's all I wanted."

As we made our way into the jungle, hand-in-hand-in-hand, I could have sworn I heard the gods laughing.

Midnight Laundry

Patrick sidled over to the plush chair where the vampire was curled with a book, pulling over an ottoman so he could sit near her. She didn't look up from her novel, so after staring at her for a few seconds, he finally spoke.

"You're a vampire, aren't you?" His voice cracked and he winced in embarrassment.

The vampire's eyes swiveled up to meet his over the top of her book. Her pale irises appeared to float unanchored in the whites of her eyes, surrounded only by the faintest impression of milky blue.

"I never thought I'd run into one of you at old Suds 'n Java, but I guess vampires have to wash their clothes, too." He waited for a response.

The woman's eerie eyes slid slowly back to the pages of her novel. He noted that, as he had suspected from across the room, she was definitely not breathing. Now that he was sitting so close to her he could really see how pale and papery her skin was, too, so translucent the fluorescent lights illuminated purple veins crisscrossing beneath the surface. She smelled vaguely of clove cigarettes.

Patrick opened his mouth to speak again, but a washing machine buzzed. The woman was sitting in her chair one moment, and the next all that remained of her was a novel flat on the seat. When he glanced at the machines, she was removing clothes from a washer. A shiver ran down his spine at this inhuman display of quickness. *She could probably kill me in an instant*, he realized, his jeans tightening.

Despite his better judgment, he got up and made his way to the washing machines under the pretense of checking his own clothes. The vampire moved at normal speed now, pulling her black garments apart and tossing them into a dryer.

"Do you use that special detergent for black clothes?" He tried out his most charming smile. "You could probably get a lot of use out of it."

She didn't even glance at him. She fed the machine some quarters and returned, at a deliberate pace, to her plush chair.

Patrick cursed under his breath as he transferred his own wet items from the washer to the dryer. He was clearly not impressing her, but he stubbornly wouldn't let himself be discouraged.

Patrick thought he was a decently handsome man. He was skinny, sure, but he had the lean muscles of a former high school wrestler. He regretted not showering that day, because his face was scruffy and he wore a battered baseball cap to cover his oily hair. He discreetly checked his armpits--he was wearing the same flannel shirt he'd been wearing all week--and found the odor to be musky and masculine, strong but not offensive. He'd had a girlfriend once who loved the smell of unwashed man, and ever since he'd kept his deodorant-wearing to a minimum, hoping to find another girl who was just as much an animal in the sack.

His hands, were, of course, a problem; few women found rough calluses and huge, knobby fingers to be sexy. His knuckles were red and cracked, and here and there his fingers were stained with paint or lacquer. He was, however, proud to be a working man, especially after that time he'd spent in the penitentiary, and he wore the stains and scars proudly, a sign of his success despite the odds stacked against him.

At this moment, however, he swiped his hands on his jeans self-consciously. He hoped she wouldn't notice. Maybe vampires didn't care about that sort of thing.

He looked back to the lounge area where she was seated, her legs slung over the armrest so she could recline sideways in the chair. She would have been pretty enough if she'd been mortal, but the fact of her immortality made her irresistible. Patrick made his way back to the chair, seating himself on the ottoman beside her once more. He watched her expectantly.

She looked up at him over her book again, this time with her sandy-blonde eyebrows drawn together in a scowl.

"Is it true you can read minds?" He tried to sound conversational.

She regarded him, unblinking, and made no reply. With a start, he realized that she might be trying to communicate with him telepathically. Closing his eyes, Patrick imagined them kissing, their tongues writhing together passionately.

When he returned from his reverie, she was ignoring him again, engrossed once more in her book.

Anger boiled in Patrick's stomach. This might be his only chance to ever be with a vampire, and the target of his affections was not even giving him a chance. Furious, he stood and snatched the novel from her.

Her hands remained poised, as if she still held the book, but her eyes had flicked up to his face. "*Now* will you listen to me? I'm trying to--"

Icy cold fingers closed around his throat, lifting him off the ground. From below him, the vampire growled, her mouth opening to reveal multiple rows of teeth: sharp, triangular, and made specifically to rip through flesh. Her free hand grabbed the book, tossing it onto the chair behind her.

A voice simmered up from the depths of her belly, unnaturally low and echoing in the quiet of the empty laundromat. "Will you *please* let me read?"

She released him. His knees buckled when he hit the ground and he toppled sideways. When he had recovered himself and stood, he looked back to see the vampire seated once more, novel again held in her pale hands.

Humiliated, Patrick stalked out of the laundromat, hunching his shoulders and shoving his hands into his pockets. He hoped she would be gone if he returned for his laundry in a few hours. As he stumped along, he wondered about the nearest watering hole where he could drown his sorrow.

He supposed that he could always go to the werewolf bar.

Shadows of the Darkest Jade

Satindra and I followed the Silk Road out of Gandhara and down into the plains of the Empire of Han, surrounded by merchants and travelers. The people we met along the Indus River, even many miles beyond prosperous Gandhara, recognized our saffron robes and gave generously to our alms bowls. We sat at their fires night after night, welcomed guests. In exchange for food and a warm place to sleep, Satindra told them of the *dharma*, mediated their disputes, and blessed them with his quiet strength. I knew, as I sat listening to him retell the tales I had heard a hundred times, the Guru had chosen wisely when he sent Satindra among the Han, for he had the calm charisma and sagely demeanor that befit a true disciple of Amitabha Buddha.

As we journeyed, the number of other travelers on the road began to dwindle. Eventually, we left the great Silk Road and walked into unknown territory. The road narrowed and wound its way through expanses of rice paddies, where stoop-shouldered peasants laboured in the hot sun.

Unfortunately, the people of the Han Empire had rarely seen monks and, even more rarely, begging monks, and did not know what to make of us, especially as one of us was a foreigner and the other was barely a man, then unable to grow a beard. When we brought out our alms bowls, they scoffed, made offensive remarks about beggars, and some even spat on the ground at our feet. We ran out of our carefully preserved rice ration within a few days of leaving the Silk Road, and were so hungry our steps began to falter.

"Brother Satindra," I said reluctantly as we trudged through another hot, dusty day. "We must find food." I meant to imply we should steal what we could not beg, though I could not bring myself to suggest it outright.

Satindra nodded. "Amitabha will provide," he said, with perfect faith, never indicating whether he understood my hidden meaning. "The Guru sent us here to bring the *dharma*; Amitabha will provide."

I'm ashamed to say I lost faith, but Satindra never stopped believing. Even as we staggered up to a small, bamboo-and-mud hut, so exhausted we could barely stand, he drew his alms bowl from his robes and said the traditional words of blessing in a voice weak with hunger. The smell of the evening meal drifted out to us, a scent so tantalizing I moaned aloud.

The girl who came to the door of the hut could have been my sister. She was small and golden-skinned, her jet-black hair tied modestly at the nape of her neck.

She wore the simple, cotton garments of all the Han peasants. Her narrow eyes - so like mine! - grew wide, and she turned and ran back into the house, calling to her elders in the local dialect.

I groaned again, this time sure of defeat, certain that we would be turned away and meet our deaths on the dusty road. Satindra turned and looked at me, a smile curving his chapped lips, and said "Have faith, little Brother."

The girl returned with two women, one hugely pregnant woman the other a small and elderly with a round, plump face. Both women immediately ushered us into the hut, without any questions or explanations, and just like that, we were saved and Satindra's faith was proven.

The girl's name was Jun. The pregnant woman was her mother Bao-Yu and the elderly woman was Jun's grandmother, Grandmother Mei. The men of the household were off drinking rice wine and gambling, Grandmother Mei said, so the women could do what they liked, including feeding wandering monks. She explained all this while we eagerly devoured rice and what I can honestly say was the most delicious hot soup I've ever eaten. Grandmother Mei chattered throughout the meal, gesturing with her small, shriveled hands, squinting at us with her beady, black eyes and smiling a toothless grin. Unfamiliar with the local dialect,

I only understood about half of what she said and poor Satindra, who spoke only the scholarly language of the Han and none of the rough dialects of the peasants, understood nothing. Nevertheless, we nodded enthusiastically and tried to be a good audience.

Finally, when our appetites were sated, Grandmother Mei asked us to tell our story.

"You will have to excuse Brother Satindra," I said. "He only speaks the scholar's tongue."

"Your accent is strange," Grandmother Mei said, squinting at me over her plum-like cheeks.

"I was raised in a village near here," I said, "but I have been away for many years. I remember very little."

She nodded, sitting back on her pillow, and repeated her request for our story.

I obliged as best I could, using words from the scholar's tongue and the dialect of my village interchangeably. This seemed surprisingly effective.

"We are monks from a monastery in the nation of Gandhara," I told her. "Satindra is gifted with languages and I was born in Han, so our Guru thought it would be wise to send us to spread the word of the *dharma* here. We have walked a long time, seeking the village where I was born. I don't remember the way, because I was very young when I left home."

Grandmother Mei snorted. "Why did your parents send you away? A healthy, strapping young boy?"

"I was told later, when I was older, that I was sent away because my family was so large my parents were unable to feed all of us."

The old woman nodded sagely, her head bobbing on her neck. "A few years ago, there was drought. I remember well, there were many families whose children starved." She clucked her tongue at the misfortune of it all. "Your parents were farmers, then?"

"Yes. My father and mother both worked in the rice fields. I remember four brothers and one sister, but there may be others, who were sent away like me, or who were born since I left."

"You should be grateful your mother sent you to live with the monks," Grandmother Mei chided me, perhaps hearing some sorrow in my voice when I spoke of my family. "She saved you from a life of backbreaking work, toil and sorrow. Instead, you have learned to read and write, haven't you? And now you travel the world!" She snorted. "It's a lucky thing for you. I only wish that little Jun were a boy so we could send her with you, away from this life."

I looked at Jun, who blushed and looked away. "Some say that the Amitabha Buddha's most dedicated disciples were his wife and consorts," Satindra volunteered, speaking slowly in the scholarly language of the Han nobles.

Grandmother Mei guffawed her skepticism. "The

day women are allowed to become monks will be the day we learn to piss standing up!" She laughed wildly, slapping her small hand against her thigh. Bao-Yun and Jun looked uncomfortable, but smiled obediently at the old woman's coarse joke. Wheezing with laughter, Grandmother Mei requested tea and little Jun hopped up and began preparing tea for all of us.

"Tell me more about your Amitabha," Grandmother Mei demanded and, while Jun ground tea leaves and boiled water, Satindra and I did our best to explain the *dharma*.

While we talked, Jun placed an earthenware bowl of tea in her grandmother's hands, and the old woman sipped and made appreciative sounds. "It's too bad neither of you needs a wife; little Jun is an expert tea-maker, already, and she is barely ten years old! Think what a woman she will be in just a few years!"

Satindra and I blushed and looked at the floor. Some orders of Ambitabha's followers took consorts, but ours did not; we were humble monks dedicated to poverty and chastity. Grandmother Mei chuckled at our modest reaction to her words and said, "Did your mother make tea like this, Little Brother?"

"You should call me Wen, Grandmother Mei," I replied. "And yes, she did. I remember the scent of it." And it was true: the scent of the mint leaves crushed with the tea leaves brought back memories of my childhood and the bamboo house where I slept chest-to-back with my brothers.

"Then the village of your birth is near here, Brother Wen. You will always know what part of the Han Empire you're in by the taste of the tea, because the leaves taste different and are prepared differently wherever you go." She took another sip and sighed contentedly.

My memories stirred as Jun placed a bowl of tea in my own hands. The minty scent and warmth of the pottery clasped in my hands brought me back to that dark, warm bamboo hut with my family. "I don't remember much about the village, not even the name," I said softly. "But I do remember a festival, where we burned offerings of tea leaves like this...the festival of the Jade Crane."

Grandmother Mei threw up her hands so quickly her tea bowl dropped to the floor, spilling hot liquid across the dirt floor. She shrieked something unintelligible and the eyes she turned to me were no longer sparkling with kindness and amusement, but rather were full of fear and loathing. Her toothless mouth opened, a black cavern, and she made a loud keening sound that raised the hairs on my arms. The change was so abrupt I had no time to react; no one did. We all just stared at Grandmother Mei for a moment, baffled.

Then the little girl and her mother took action. Bao-Yun put her arms around her mother and began speaking calmly to her, so that gradually, the keening subsided to a low moan. It was still a terrible sound, like the squalling of an infant. Jun, meanwhile, collected the tea bowls from me and Satindra, and hustled us out of the house.

"What did you say?" Satindra asked, as Jun pushed us from the hut.

"I only said there was a festival in my village," I replied. "The festival of the Jade - "

I could not finish this thought, because Grandmother Mei began to shriek again, and little Jun pressed one small hand against my mouth. She shook her head fervently, her narrow eyes so wide I could see the whites all around her black irises. She pushed us both out of the hut and down the road a little ways, and then ran back into the house.

Satindra and I stood in the dark road for a few minutes, listening to Grandmother Mei's terrified wailing. It had all happened so quickly. We stared at each other numbly, then placed our alms bowls back into our robes and began to move down the road, away from the house.

Eventually, the wailing stopped and we heard the sound of footsteps. We turned to see Jun running toward us, a small bag of uncooked rice in her arms. Wordlessly, she pressed the bag into my hands. Her eyes were full of fear, but also compassion, and I thanked her for the generous donation. Then I said, "What did your grandmother say when I mentioned...the bird?"

Jun frowned, licked her lips, and glanced back at the hut, where the firelight spilled out of the open doorway and onto the road. "'Cursed'," she said, in a whisper, and the wind seemed to steal the word from her mouth, so it did not linger, but was whisked away into the night, so it almost seemed unreal. I wanted her to repeat it, so I could be sure of what she had said, but instead, she turned and ran back to the house.

"'Cursed'?" Satindra repeated. "Does that mean what I think it means?"

"Yes," I replied.

To my surprise, Satindra laughed, drawing one arm around my shoulders and patting my back. "Don't let a superstitious old woman frighten you, Little Brother. Cursed. Ha! If anything, we are blessed. Let's find a field where we can spend the night."

We slept under the stars that night and, though I glowered, Satindra remained in high spirits. He detailed the reasons we were lucky: before her fit, Grandmother Mei had blessed us with a generous meal and a chance to share the *dharma*; the evening was a pleasant temperature, and no storm clouds threatened to interrupt our sleep with rain; we had not been robbed or set upon by criminals; and we knew that soon, we would arrive in the village of my birth, and perhaps even find my family.

Two wandering monks could hardly want for more, he said, as we bedded down in a cow field.

The following day, I was melancholic, having slept fitfully. Our morning meditation, where we chanted a mantra as we walked, brought me no comfort. During the hottest part of the day, we rested. Satindra cooked a little of the rice Jun had given us and we ate it slowly, savoring every grain. It tasted slightly of mint and the flavor brought me a confusing jumble of memories.

When we walked on the Silk Road, we passed many shrines to local gods. Some of the richest had been statues carved of jade or ivory, housed in pagodas and tended by priests. Travelers had laid offerings of milk, honey, rice, and even meat at these shrines. As we left the main road, the size of the altars became less impressive. Every day or so, we passed one of these little shrines, usually with a tiny, crude stone likeness of some god or another, or simply a collection of pebbles meant to be a marker. There were usually the remains of meager offerings at these smaller shrines, or no offerings at all, because so few travelers passed them.

Now, as we walked farther from the Silk Road and Grandmother Mei's house, the character of these shrines changed. Though we had ignored the altars previously, I now felt compelled to look at the small statues. The other shrines along this country road had been simple cairns or had little hand-carved animals made of a common stone or wood, something that would have no value to thieves. But the afternoon after our encounter with Grandmother Mei, we passed a shrine with a statuette, carved with great detail, out of what appeared to be some kind of jade.

I crouched in front of the shrine, staring at the dark statuette it housed in what might have been half of a huge, stone bowl, turned on its side. The little statue was black, and mostly in shadow, but when the sunlight hit it just right, it looked green, like the darkest jade. The details of the statue were difficult to discern, but the shape was not human, nor that of any animal I had seen before. I got the impression of bulbous eyes and an elongated head and many arms, like the Hindu goddess Kali, but no matter how I squinted, I could not determine the exact features of the statue. Finally, thinking that perhaps my fingers could make sense of what perplexed my eyes, I reached out and ran my fingers over the stone.

I expected the cool hardness of jade, but instead, the stone was warm, perhaps from the sunlight, and the texture was wet and slippery. I jerked my hand away and looked at my fingers, expecting them to be wet; they were dry, though the sensation of the oily stone remained. I didn't want to touch the thing again and couldn't stand looking at it, so I backed away from the shrine and hurried to catch up to Satindra, who squatted further down the road, waiting for me.

"What's wrong, Little Brother?" he asked as I joined him, still staring at my fingers. They felt tainted, somehow, as if I had touched something unclean. I had the urge to wipe them on my robes.

"There is something wrong with the statue in that shrine," I told him, scowling.

Satindra chuckled. "I think today you're determined to find something wrong with everything," he replied.

Thinking that perhaps he was correct, I sighed and resigned myself to our daily trudge.

We walked for several days more, each day passing more of the shrines with the black-green soapstone idols. The road became increasingly pitted and overgrown with weeds, narrowing down to almost nothing, but the shrines seemed only to grow larger, each statue taller than the last.

Even stranger, the number of people we saw along the road dwindled as the idols to the local god grew larger. The fields once full of workers were now empty, the rice overgrown and unkempt, as if the crops had simply been forgotten. The fields that had once gone on forever now ended in forest, and the forest was reclaiming those fields.

Eventually, we came upon some simple bamboo huts much like Grandmother Mei's, but these were empty and beyond them, the forest was dark and forbidding. The remains of cooking fires were still smoldering, in some cases, and half-finished cups of tea sat beside dirty rice bowls swarming with ants. After investigating one of these houses, I turned to Satindra and said, "It's as if everyone has just disappeared. This is unnatural. I don't like it."

Satindra tried to laugh off my fears with his usual grace, but failed. His laughter sounded hollow and misplaced in the silent, empty village. "Don't worry, Brother Wen. I'm sure there's some explanation. We should find a place to sleep."

Though we were not superstitious men, Satindra and I did not sleep in the village. We ate the last of our rice in a field nearby, where we could see the huts without being too close to them.

Every night since Grandmother Mei's, I had slept poorly, my dreams fraught with screaming old women and huge black birds with sharply curved beaks. Now the birds dripped oil and opened their mouths to shriek with Grandmother Mei's raspy voice, "Cursed! Cursed!" I woke in the night, sweating and tangled in my robes. I looked about for Satindra and found him crouched beside me, awake and alert despite the late hour. His eyes were so wide I could see the whites even in the darkness that shrouded us.

I followed his gaze to the abandoned village.

There were lights moving among the previously empty huts. I started to say something to him, to suggest that we go speak with the villagers, but he silenced me with a hand squeezing my arm. Never had I seen him like this, with every nerve taut and straining, so I bit my tongue. After some time, the lights moved away and Satindra turned to me.

His eyes looked doubly huge with his face so dark. The night around us was eerily silent, not even the wind stirring the fallow rice fields. "I don't think those were people," he whispered.

"What do you mean?" I replied, squatting beside him in the dirt so we were almost at eye-level.

"I saw their faces. They didn't look right." He shook his head emphatically.

"What did you see?"

Satindra swallowed hard, as if something large and ill-tasting were caught in his throat. His huge eyes remained fixed on my face, unblinking and intense. "'*Dakini*'."

Dakini is an ancient word that refers to an otherworldly, inhuman being: a god or a demon.

"We should go," I said.

To my horror, Satindra shook his head. "No," he said firmly. Though his hands were shaking, he stood, his eyes still fixed unswervingly on me. "This is why we were sent here, Brother Wen. Your people need to hear the *dharma*. The Guru sent us here to free your people."

I shook my head and stood up, too. Satindra was a full head taller than I, so I still stared up at him. "No, Brother Satindra! The Guru could not have foreseen this! We cannot go alone; it's too dangerous. We should return to the monastery...."

He interrupted me by gripping my arms hard and giving me a little shake, as one would a hysterical woman. "You would dare to question the enlightened Guru?" He released me abruptly and I staggered back.

Satindra whirled away from me and walked resolutely toward the village.

I watched him for a few moments, debating what to do. The night air seemed to rush into the space left by Satindra's quick departure, enveloping me in dark, cool silence. And then, beyond the quiet of the abandoned village and the overgrown fields, I heard a sound, faint but persistent. At first, I couldn't identify it. Then I thought it was the buzzing of insects. Finally, I realized that it was human voices, chanting a repetitive mantra.

I ran after Satindra.

The tracks of the *dakini* were easy to follow; they had not bothered to hide their movements, and we followed their trail of muddy footprints and broken branches deep into the dark, dense forest, where trees and bushes tugged at our robes and we tripped over huge roots. Here, we lost the trail, the darkness was too omnipresent, but now we could hear the chanting and the high-pitched, frantic notes of a zither.

The chanting people were in the center of a clearing, where they sang in the darkness without benefit of a fire. I couldn't see the zither-player in the darkness, but I knew he was off to the right somewhere, because I could hear the slithering, off-key notes. He played no tune, just as the chant seemed to have no rhythm. I had thought that perhaps, upon approaching the chanters, we'd be able to discern their words, but I realized, as we grew closer, the words were gibberish, meaningless, though they repeated them with conviction.

In the dim moonlight, we could see the villagers were mostly naked, though a few still wore shreds of clothing. They were turned away from us, kneeling on the ground, facing something at the center of the clearing. I had to peek around Satindra's bulk to get a glimpse of them - it was impossible to walk two abreast in the close forest - but I could see that a few were dancing ecstatically to the tuneless music. The din was horrible and I covered my ears to drown out what I could. It made me feel confused and hopeless, as if the veil between sanity and insanity could be breached by this combination of sounds.

There was a stench that made my eyes water. It smelled like rotten meat, sour milk, feces, and blood, all together. I fought the urge to vomit.

Satindra stopped in front of me and I ran into his back. He had stopped moving completely and I clawed at him, trying to make him move so I could see the people in the clearing, but he was frozen in place. Standing on my toes, gripping his shoulder, I was able to see a little around him, where the moonlight illuminated the dancers. For a moment, I saw with terrible clarity the twisted bodies, arms and limbs akimbo in unnatural positions, scattered on the ground. Among them were the tiny feet of children and the gnarled hands of the arthritic elderly. The dancers moved around and on top of these motionless forms, naked bodies gyrating horribly, eyes wide and mouths distorted.

Beyond the dancers was the thing they worshiped. It was so tall it blotted out the stars behind it, dwarfing the huge trees, and I squinted to make out its features. Was that a long, crane-like neck or arms? Was that a deformed head or a stooped back? Like the statues in the altars along the road, it was a thing that could not be seen completely, as if it undulated without moving.

Suddenly, Satindra turned and wrapped his arms around me, crushing me to his chest. His hand held my head against his shoulder. He mumbled something as he held me hard against his robes. I didn't struggle at first, thinking that perhaps he was frightened and hugging me against him in fear, but soon, I ran out of breath. Crushed against his chest, I could not inhale, so I fought him. Taller and stronger than I, Satindra won easily and, as I thrashed against him, he chanted softly in my ear, "Don't look, Little Brother. Don't look at it!"

I awoke some time later back in the village. Satindra sat beside me, guarding me from the possessed villagers lest they return, his eyes wide and unblinking as he stared into the darkness. When I asked him how long I had been unconscious, whether we should go back to the monastery, whether we had any food, his only reply was to repeat his bleak chant: "Don't look, Little Brother. Don't look at it!"

These were the only words Satindra spoke throughout our journey back to the monastery in Gandhara. The trek was dismal, now that Satindra was no longer an inspirational young monk, but instead, a mad, sorrowful man who sometimes screamed at strangers and other times, wept uncontrollably for hours. The weather turned foul and we trudged through mud up to our calves. We both grew pathetically scrawny, bones showing through our skin, but the other travelers shunned us because Satindra still moaned his disturbing mantra. We survived on will alone and the rare, meager donations of those truly generous followers of Amitabha who knew their duty, even if the monks to whom they gave alms were dirty and mad.

We barely survived that return journey and arrived on the Guru's doorstep shells of our former selves.

The Guru could get nothing sensible out of Satindra, of course, so eventually, he came to me to ask what had befallen us in the terrible wilds of the Empire of Han. I could make no words in reply.

Now, knowing that death awaits me soon, at last, I can write about the events that occurred, though they seem like a fever-dream after so many years. Even now, however, there are parts of the story I can't reveal, which I will take to the funeral pyre. These horrors destroyed poor Brother Satindra, who died muttering his cursed phrase to the last, mere days after our arrival in Gandhara. He left me alone to carry the burden of the horror and now, at last, I will be free of it, for perhaps in death, I will at last no longer see the jade crane when I close my eyes, blotting out the stars with its vastness, or hear the chanting of the mad acolytes dancing naked at its feet. There was a time when I sought the peace of enlightenment, but now I seek only the silence of death, where these terrors may be obliterated in nothingness.

Saffron Skies

I knew we were doomed when the sun rose and dark shapes materialized from the misty sea below the airship, resolving themselves into buildings and bridges. There was an inherent wrongness about the structures, though I couldn't tell you precisely why. Perhaps it was the green-black stone from which they were constructed, the way it gleamed like sweat-slick skin in the hazy dawn light. Perhaps it was their odd placement, the strange angles of their corners and edges, or their monolithic size. Or perhaps it was the fishy reek of the city itself, so powerful that I covered my face with my handkerchief and breathed the musty scent of old sweat instead.

"Captain?" Zhoigar asked from her place at the helm. "That doesn't look like Bangladesh."

"Where's the spyglass?"

Champo appeared at my elbow, spyglass

extended. His young face was creased with worry.

I drew the instrument to my eye. Once magnified, I could see the city's wide avenues were crowded with kelp, dead fish, and stranger things. "Nothing's moving. The city's dead. But..."

"But what, Captain?" Champo's voice had only recently changed to more manly timbre, and now it cracked.

"It's all...wrong. There's seaweed in the streets, like the whole city came up out of the ocean." As if in response, the city pulsed, like it was breathing, and I experienced the powerful urge to abandon my airship and leap to my death on the rock below. I could almost feel the cool ocean breeze against my back as I fell, cartwheeling to my demise.

Swallowing hard, I shoved the urge down into my belly. I lowered the spyglass and stepped away from the railing, turning my back to it.

"Could it be Shambhala?" Zhoigar's words were hushed, reverent.

"No. This is no city of enlightenment."

Champo glanced back at the pair of warships looming behind us. "The Chinese aren't turning back."

"Then we can't either."

"We'll run out of fuel," Zhoigar observed, tapping the fuel gage with one scarred knuckle.

"There's no fuel down there." I gestured to the city beneath our feet. Though I was turned away from the railing, I could sense the city beckoning to me. My stomach lurched.

Champo reached for the spyglass. "Let me look."

"No!" I yanked the instrument from his seeking fingers. "No one is to look."

Both pilot and lookout stared at me, their eyes wide. I slipped the spyglass into my pocket. "I'll go inform the monks. Hold steady on our present course."

Zhoigar scowled. "Like I have a choice." She was right, of course; we'd had no choice since the rudder had been blasted to pieces by a Chinese cannonball hours before.

I didn't reply, choosing instead to leave the deck as quickly as possible. As I descended into the ship's interior, I felt as though I were being watched. Chill bumps rose on my arms.

In the cargo hold, thirteen monks huddled among the supplies. I searched their faces for the familiar visage of the Dalai Lama. They all wore the same saffron robes, with the same close-cropped black hair and round, brown faces. None of them wore Tenzin Gyatso's characteristic glasses. Though I was Tibetan by birth, I was no Buddhist then, and had never paid enough attention to know the Dalai Lama's features by heart. I approached the eldest monk instead.

"We've come through the fog. We should be over the open ocean but...there's a city, covered in seaweed as if it rose from the ocean floor."

The other monks gasped and whispered among themselves. I heard the word "Shambhala." The eldest monk held out his hand and clasped it in mine, smiling. His skin was smooth and soft, so soft I could have punctured it with my fingernail without applying pressure. I imagined his blood flowing over my fingers and jerked back.

"Not Shambhala," I told them. "It's a city that shouldn't be. It's unnatural...wrong somehow."

One of the youngest monks came forward. "Why are you telling us this?"

I squinted at him. Could he be Tenzin Gyatso? "I thought you should know: The Chinese are still pursuing us. Eventually we're going to run out of fuel."

"But you told us the Chinese were going to run out of fuel first."

I nodded. "Yes, well, they haven't. Not yet anyway. We're still holding out hope they'll run out before we do. They should have already, somewhere over Bangladesh."

The other monks hissed and began yammering, but the young one held up a hand and they silenced. "What happens should we run out of fuel before the Chinese do?"

"We'll land the *Basundhara* on the ocean."

"And?" The boy could not have been more than twenty years old, but his gaze was steady and confident, more like that of an older man than some young upstart.

"And then we'll be boarded by the Chinese, assuming they choose not to destroy the ship completely and leave us all to drown." I averted my gaze, suddenly ashamed. "I'm sorry, Your Holiness."

The young man chuckled. "Call me Gyatso, please. Why this sudden respect? I know you only took us on for the money. You're not a religious man, you told us so yourself."

I met his eyes. "That was before the city."

He sobered instantly. "Take me to see."

"No. No one should look at it."

"I want to see, Captain Dorje." His tone was one of authority, one that permitted no argument.

I turned and made my way back to the deck, and the Dalai Lama followed.

Fog still clung to the *Basundhara* in tendrils here

and there, illuminated by the rising sun. Gyatso's robes were a warm orange in the murky yellow light. I brought him to the helm, simultaneously terrified and thrilled that I was now within view of the strange city.

"This is my pilot, Zhoigar, and my lookout, Champo." I prompted them both to bow. "We're blessed to have the Dalai Lama on board."

Champo bowed low, but Zhoigar barely nodded her head. "I thought we were transporting a decoy," she growled.

"I'm afraid not," Gyatso replied, smiling.

Zhoigar frowned but went to her post. I'd never seen my hot-headed pilot retreat from a fight before and felt my respect for the young monk grow.

Gyatso went to the railing and looked down at the city sprawled below us. We watched him in silence, waiting for his reaction. I fingered the spyglass in my pocket, wondering whether I should offer it to him, resisting the urge to peer through the lens myself. The city called to me with a siren's song, and I studied the others, trying to judge from their expressions whether they heard the same terrible music.

Finally, after a long, deliberate silence, Gyatso spoke over his shoulder to me. "I see what you mean."

"What is it?" Zhoigar asked.

"I don't know. But it's not Shambhala. It's the opposite of Shambhala."

"How can you stand to look at it?" I asked, keeping my own distance from the railing.

The Dalai Lama threw me a smile. "Once a man has wrestled with his inner demons, he can wrestle anything, Captain." He glanced over the starboard railing and eyed the Chinese warships.

Zhoigar and I followed his gaze. Both warships were four times the size of the *Basundhara*. Each was painted white on its underside and black on its topside, and each ship's prow was decorated to resemble a Fu Dog. The cannons that lolled from the sides like stumpy legs were carved into whiskered dragons. Massive engines churned so loudly we could hear them humming from hundreds of feet away, even under the engines of the *Basundhara*. And the deck of each ship teamed with armed soldiers dressed in regimental black, tiny as ants at this distance, but far more dangerous.

If we allowed the Chinese to catch us, the Dalai Lama would be taken prisoner, and the rest of us would likely be killed. Or maybe enslaved. Still, that fate was more appealing to me in that moment than landing on the green-black rock of the impossible city.

I heard a soft scuffling and turned to find Champo with one leg over the railing, climbing overboard.

"No!" I lunged for him. He leaped; I grabbed his shirt. Zhoigar and Gyatso gripped his arms and we hauled the boy back onto the deck. As we pulled, he thrashed, trying to wriggle free of his tunic. His mouth twisted unnaturally and his eyes were fever-bright. And he made a sound, a terrible sound, a keening like nothing I'd ever heard before.

The moment he was on the deck and we relaxed,

he wrenched himself free and made for the railing again, shrieking gibberish. Zhoigar and I grabbed at him, but he writhed free of our hands, leaped up onto the railing, and flung himself overboard.

We followed him and stood gasping at the railing, watching in helpless horror as the screaming boy spun toward the city below. His wailing was eventually drowned out by the ship's engines as he became no larger than a miniscule black mote.

A faint sound reached my ears in the relative quiet that followed. It was much like the garbled wailing Champo had uttered only moments before. I looked back at the Chinese warship to starboard just in time to see a tiny figure launch itself from the deck, tumbling through the air, end over end. He was followed by another, and another.

"What's happening?" Zhoigar cried in a terrified warble.

"It's the city. It's calling to them! We should tie ourselves down."

The Dalai Lama said a prayer while we went
to find rope. The call of the city was growing louder in
my head, so loud it even subsumed the sound of the
Basundhara's engines. "We need to hurry," I told Zhoigar,
pressing my hands against my ears. The attempt to block
out the maddening call was futile. It was inside my head,
pulsing and itching, and the only way to end the agony
was to leap overboard and join Champo on the slick rock
hundreds of feet below....

I found myself against the railing. Gyatso's hands
were on my shoulders; Zhoigar worked frantically to
secure a rope about my waist.

There was a sound like a thunderclap. The city
below us began to tremble, then quake. I craned my
neck to watch as a long, jagged crack appeared down the
middle of buildings and streets and bridges alike, as if
they were all carved from the same giant piece of stone
that was now splitting apart.

"What is that?" Zhoigar whispered.

Staring back at us from the darkness within that

long, terrible crack was a massive eye. It reminded me of the eye of a whale, huge and black, surrounded by wrinkled, blubbery lids--only larger. Impossibly so, and implying that the monster below the city was the size of the city itself, larger than any creature that ever existed upon the Earth. The eye reflected back an image of the golden morning and the airships hovering above it, as if the creature within were soulless and existed only to those it reflected.

Something dark exploded from the crack and wrapped itself around the port warship. It lashed the ship from stem to stern, sweeping black-clad soldiers from the deck. The Chinese fought back, the sharp report of their pistols and the lower *boom* of their cannons echoing back to us.

"A tentacle," The Dalai Lama remarked under his breath.

A second tentacle appeared, hovering above the *Basundhara* and casting a long, twisted shadow upon the deck. Zhoigar screamed. I struggled with the ropes to draw my pistol, then took haphazard aim and fired. Zhoigar regained her senses and did the same, firing again and again until our weapons were empty. The monstrous appendage shrank back, disappearing.

Zhoigar ran to the helm to reload. I clawed desperately at the ropes, trying to free myself. "Help me!" I called to the Dalai Lama.

Gyatso laid one hand against my forehead and met my eyes. His expression was utterly serene, as if the carnage around us were imagined. "Om mani padme hum," he chanted.

"Om mani padme hum," I replied, rolling the sounds on my lips, in my mind. As I repeated the words a sense of calm enveloped me, my panic melting away. "Pilot Zhoigar, get us out of here."

Zhoigar grabbed the wheel and spun it hard, to no effect, and cursed our blasted rudder. "Give it gas!" I commanded, hoping our lighter ship could outrun the monster as the heavier warships could not.

The tentacles attacked the starboard warship next.

This time, three of the horrible appendages worked in tandem to crush the ship and thrash it back and forth like a dog worrying a dead bird, flinging uniformed soldiers this way and that like loosened feathers.

Zhoigar sobbed, crouching behind the wheel in abject terror. "They're coming for us!"

I couldn't count all the tentacles that descended upon us then. They were so huge and numerous they blotted out the sun as they swarmed the ship. One closed around my arm, slimy and rubbery and stinking of rotten fish, pulling hard enough to rend my limb from the socket. A second tentacle encircled the Dalai Lama mere feet from me, lifting him from the deck. He never cried out or flailed, just quietly allowed himself to be squeezed. His expression was calm, accepting, peaceful. I saw his lips move, reciting his mantra, though the words were lost under my own screams.

The ropes binding the balloon to the *Basundhara* creaked in protest as the tentacles attacked the balloon, yanking hard. The cleats fastening the ropes to the deck gave way, one by one, bursting from the wood like shots from cannon. The tentacles ripped the balloon from the ship, rendering us earthbound, and then tossed the balloon into the air like a toy.

A golden light emanated from behind the Dalai Lama's head, catching my attention so I turned to regard him through tear-hazed vision. The light started as the merest hint of sunlight, and grew gradually to an aura, then a beacon.

The tentacle gripping him dissolved in the magical light. A roar shook the *Basundhara*. Released, I sagged against the ropes that bound me. Moving as one, all the tentacles disappeared over the sides, slinking away as if trying to hide from the blazing beacon. I looked down to see the eye retreating from the crack. Waves rushed up over the city, the ocean reclaiming it.

Our balloon torn away and the tentacles gone, the *Basundhara* fell. In the split second before we crashed, Tenzin Gyatso stood alone on the deck, his head bowed and hands pressed together. Smiling.

We hit the water so hard I blacked out.

I roused the next morning, when an Indian patrol ship found us floating in the ocean like so much flotsam. Two of the monks had been killed in the crash, one crushed by cargo and the other, who had thought to help us on the deck, lost overboard. Several others were badly injured, but Zhoigar and Gyatso had tended their wounds and most would recover--from their physical injuries, at least.

For two days and two nights we were towed to shore. At night I could hear men screaming in their sleep. I lay awake because I, too, was wracked with nightmares. The throbbing of my dislocated shoulder worsened in the dark, as well, bringing to mind the pulsing of the impossible city. I wondered how long it would remain dormant beneath the waves. I shuddered at the memory of the colossal, gleaming eye.

Zhoigar came to find me in my quarters when at last we docked on the third day. "It's time to deboard, Captain. How are you feeling?"

"Much better. Here." I pushed a leather map case into her hands.

"What's this?"

"The deed to the *Basundhara*. I know she's seen better days, but with the money the monks paid us for transport you should be able to get her up and running again."

"What? No. I don't want it. Not without you."

"Either you take it or I'm giving it to the first person I see when I step on the dock. I'm going to join the Karmapa Order." I'd been considering these words for days, and saying them aloud gave my choice the ring of finality.

I daresay Zhoigar heard the same ring. She stared at me for several long seconds, lips pursed, and when I didn't back down, she sighed. "You're sure about this?" Her eyes shone with what appeared to be genuine affection.

"You aren't going all soft on me now, are you?"

She gave me her usual wry smile. "Nah, I just

want to make sure you won't change your mind later."

I adjusted the sling that held my injured arm. "I'm sure. I've never been so sure about anything in my life."

"Airship Captain to monk. That'll be a change... but if you're sure, then I'll take over for you. I'll treat the old girl like she was my own daughter. Or mother."

"I know you will, that's why I chose you. I'll miss her...and you."

Zhoigar was never one for sentimentality. She nodded and then lifted her chin to indicate that someone was standing behind me.

I turned to find the Dalai Lama silhouetted in the doorway. His robes were crusted with brine and his face was weather-beaten from so many days at sea, but his eyes were still bright and his smile was warm. I'd never told him about my plans to abandon my airship and take a monk's vows. I'd never needed to tell him, not after what we'd endured that foggy dawn somewhere over the Indian Ocean.

He extended his hand. I took it, and I never looked back.

Frozen Souls

"Are you nervous about tomorrow, Li?" Shen asks between mouthfuls of rice.

Lien shrugs. "I've done it before." She sips her tea, watching him over the rim of the tiny porcelain cup.

"I would be scared," Shen says, trying to goad her into an embarrassing confession.

Lien knows this trick and deflects the conversation. "I know. That's why they send me instead of you."

"They send you because you're the smallest," Shen replies. This is a dance they have done before; he knows the steps.

"They send Li because he's the bravest," the ordinarily reticent Bao adds. "He volunteered, and you did not."

Lien lowers her head coyly, a show of respect whose real intent is to hide her blushing cheeks. Her affection for Bao has become bothersome. Sometimes she even thinks, when he defends her like this, that he knows her secret. Earlier today his hand brushed hers while they worked and, though he seemed not to notice, the unexpected contact drew a shuddering breath from Lien.

Her skin touching his was like an electric shock, sending a tingle to parts of her she has long ignored.

The flap of the canvas tent opens and the foreman enters. Though the crew is almost entirely Chinese, the foreman is a huge Irishman. He counts on his enormous size and grizzled appearance to intimidate his workers; he does not know that they call him *Maxì Tuán Xióng*, The Circus Bear, mocking his size, hirsutism, and the way he takes orders from the Superintendent, always ingratiatingly willing to please. Storbridge is his name, but when he enters Bao boldly says: "*Xiong*! How can we help you today?" in English.

The others stifle their laughter at the mocking name behind their teacups. Many suddenly become engrossed in their reading or chores.

"Will Li-Li be ready tomorrow?" Storbridge demands, his voice deep and rasping, with an edge of menace. Li-Li is the white man's nickname for Lien.

"Yes, Li will be ready." Bao replies, nodding to Lien. She averts her eyes, not wanting to attract the foreman's attention.

"Good. Be up at dawn so we can get to work." Storbridge lumbers back to the tent flap, a blast of freezing air rushing in as he exits.

Lien shivers, pulling the rough wool blanket closer about her shoulders.

Shen starts laughing first, and the others join him

in low, appreciative chuckles. "Bao, you are too bold!"

Bao ignores the laughter, looking at Lien. "Sounds like the blasting did not go well today."

Lien nods. "It's too cold; the rock will be too hard. But the Superintendent demands satisfaction, so the white men ignore our engineers, and the blasting will proceed."

"With our lives the ones at risk," Shen says bitterly.

"We knew the risks when we signed our contracts," Lien reminds him, but her voice is bleak and she stares sadly at her cracked and callused hands.

The tent flap opens again, and the assembled men groan and mumble about the cold as a few more workers enter. They rush to the cooking fire to warm their frostbitten hands, ill-covered in mittens full of holes. Lien counts them and finds only six.

"Where is Fa?" she asks, and there is a hard knot in her belly while she awaits the answer.

One of the men by the fire turns to her, a warm bowl of soup held in his palms to warm them. His expression is sorrowful. "He fell," he says, and the others nod somberly.

Lien tries to fight back tears. Like her, Fa was small and nimble, perfect for the dangerous work of blasting the cliffs. He had taught her the ancient Chinese art, and had been the quickest and most agile of all the dynamite-setters. She cannot believe that he simply fell. Her mind reels with conspiracy theories, but just as quickly she dismisses them. The work is dangerous, and men die blasting the tunnels for the railroad every day. It was only a matter of time before Fa, too, met his end.

She can't allow the other workers to see her tears, so she rises and hurries out of the tent with the blanket still clutched about her. She has to be stronger and braver than the others to prevent suspicion. They have seen many men perish in the grueling work on the railroad, and she has cried for those who were her friends, but always in secret.

So much of her life is a secret.

Lien finds her way through the tent city to the latrine pits, which are thankfully less noisome in the extreme cold than they are in the summer months. No one wants to venture far from the warm tents, so the men have been urinating in the snow nearby rather than make the trek to the designated area. The latrines are virtually abandoned, a silent sanctuary for her tears.

Lien takes a few moments to empty her bladder, squatting on the far side of the latrine behind some snow-covered bushes. Once relieved, she feels a little less like weeping. She stands forlornly near the pits, unwilling to return to the tent but unable to cry. She thinks of Fa and tries to mourn him as he deserves, but she has been exhausted by the sorrow of the last terrible weeks and cannot muster much beyond a few sad sniffles.

While she stands there, knee-deep in snow, waiting for the cold to leech the heat from her bones before she returns to the fire, snowflakes begin to drift down from above. There are only a few at first, spinning idly like tops, but as she watches they begin to crowd the sky, falling faster and faster. Soon the dark landscape is all but blotted out in the torrent of snow. Panicked, Lien quickly stumbles back to her tent before the snow obliterates her path and makes walking impossible. Though she is not far from her tent, she recalls vividly when several men were lost in a blizzard the first week on the mountain, found the next morning only a few feet from their dwelling, unable to find their way to safety in the disorienting whiteness.

Bao is standing at the tent flap, pulling on his boots. He looks relieved to see her. "Li! I was going to come find you. It's not safe in a storm."

Lien is touched by his concern but doesn't dare show it. "I was at the latrine," she says coolly.

"Of course," Bao replies, his mien equally icy.

Without another word they go to their cots, where Lien lies awake listening to the breathing of the sleeping men, thinking only of how she is likely to meet her death tomorrow. She whispers many prayers to the ancestors, wondering whether Fa did the same. In the wee hours she finally finds sleep, but it is a restless sleep, and she awakens many times in the night to the frightening feeling of falling from a great height.

The next morning finds Lien dangling over a cliff face in a huge basket of woven reeds. The basket is large enough to hold a man twice Lien's size, but the job is easier if the contents are as light as possible, and the dynamite takes up its share of the container. As she does every time she is lowered over a precipice, Lien eyes the dynamite in the bottom of the basket warily, knowing how volatile it is. Their hands cold, the men lowering her over the cliff with a rope are stopping and starting more than usual, and the jerking movements of the basket are giving her motion sickness reminiscent of the seasickness on the voyage from Qwangtung to California. She closes her eyes and thinks of warm summer fields full of wildflowers. She thinks of hot, soothing tea and her mother's kind smile. She thinks of Bao's brown hand brushing hers so carelessly. She thinks of anything other than the dizzying height, the bone-numbing cold, the jerking rope, and the unstable explosives.

Finally the jerking stops. She looks up at the lip of the cliff. A boy appears and gives her a hand signal. She signals back and scoots around in the basket so she can slowly tip it toward the cliff wall. She braces with her feet and knees until she is perched perilously on the side of the basket. The woven reeds creak and groan beneath her weight.

She grabs the dynamite, heedless of the danger, facing the terrifying possibility that the basket might break beneath her. The cliff face is already defiled with the marks of an explosion, and Lien shakes her head. Why would they blast the same place over and over again? She wants to cry, thinking of Fa and how her life will be wasted alongside his in this careless manner, but she marshals herself. The Chinese workers are no more valuable to their white masters than hammers or chisels—they are simply tools to do a job, interchangeable and replaceable. This is their fate—this is *her* fate.

Sighing, reluctantly resigned to her doom, she jams several dynamite sticks into the shallow crevasses of the cliff's face. Once they're secure she lights a match on her teeth, presses the match to the wicks, and drops the match without watching its descent. She takes a deep breath and observes the flames' progress with the skill of experience; this is the part of blasting that requires finesse. Timing is everything.

She silently thanks Fa for his wisdom as the wicks burn faster than usual, spurred by the cold, dry air. She presses her feet flat against the stone and then pushes with all her strength, rolling backwards so the basket tips upright again, hopefully protecting her from the blast.

The hard, frozen stone refuses to give way to the dynamite, and the explosion has only one outlet. Instead of tunneling into the cliff, the blast explodes into the open air, pushing Lien's basket away from the cliff face. Above, the men gripping the rope struggle to maintain a hold on her lifeline, the explosion yanking the rope over the edge of the precipice with such force they can't hold it for long. They cry out in dismay as the rope is torn from their protesting fingers, the pulley on the edge snapping under the pressure, the basket spinning away from the cliff and falling, taking Lien with it to the ground.

*

Lien dreams of women in bonnets and children in straw hats. She can't see their faces and their voices are strange and muffled, so that no matter how much she strains to hear their words the sounds remain elusive. They sit in the dark, clustered around a tiny fire, and around them the night is an empty, starless void. They are small and vulnerable and the children are shivering in their cotton clothes, but she can't find any blankets in the dark, and the women don't respond when she tries to tell them the children are cold. The figures and their fire seem to grow smaller and more indistinct, and then they are gone, and Lien is alone in darkness.

She wakes to warmth and light, but above her is the starless void. She realizes gradually that she is not in her tent, on her cot; she is lying on hard, frozen earth, without a blanket, and her limbs are stiff with cold. She tries to sit up and screams as pain sears through her head.

One of her legs is immobilized, and in the dim firelight she can see that it has been splinted with slender branches. It aches, and attempting to move it results in a sharp, grinding pain that takes her breath away. She must have broken it in the fall, she muses, though her thoughts are hard to grasp, slippery as eels.

She wakes again later to more light and warmth, the fire burning brightly. A few feet away on the ground she sees the shape of another person, lying prone. She slowly sits up, fighting pain in her head as she does, until she can make out some details.

"Fa?" She cries, recognizing the bruised face turned toward the fire. Fa's eyes are closed and even though she calls his name several times he does not wake. She fears for a moment that perhaps he's dead, but then sees his chest is rising and falling with slow, even breaths. His right arm and right leg have both been splinted in the same manner as hers.

With the fire burning so brightly, Lien can at last make out her surroundings. She is ensconced in a cavern with vaulted ceilings so high they're hidden in shadow. She can't determine which way is the entrance; she licks a finger and raises it high, hoping to feel the chill breeze coming off the mountains, but the air is still.

Terrified and desperate, she tries to crawl around

the fire to join Fa, hoping to find comfort beside her teacher. Constant pain sings in her head and every movement of her broken leg is excruciating. She is sobbing in agony by the time she reaches him. She grasps for one of his limp hands, and then unconsciousness swells up and over her and drags her down into darkness.

Again, Lien dreams, but this time there is a pale man at her side, ministering to her injuries. He is mumbling in some foreign tongue, so quietly she can barely make out the sounds. She tries to speak to him but her words are only gibberish, and he ignores her. She tries to make out his features but they are indistinct; she can't determine the color of his eyes or the shape of his mouth no matter how intently she focuses.

When next she wakes she is still beside Fa, but she is on her back, once again looking up at the ceiling shrouded in darkness. Beside them the fire burns low, and a copper tea kettle nestled in the flames whistles shrilly, the sound echoing in the massive cavern. Baffled, Lien looks about for the invisible caretaker who has put the kettle on the fire. The cavern remains empty and mysterious, giving up none of its secrets.

Her head protesting the whistling, Lien crawls to the fire and snatches the kettle out, barely avoiding burning her fingers. A copper cup rests beside the fire ring, and she fills it with boiling water from the kettle. The scent of coffee rises up with the steam, and Lien grimaces; she despises the American drink. She is desperate enough to drink a few mouthfuls of the bitter brew, however, much as she detests the strong flavor.

Next she pours coffee for Fa, and awkwardly--ignoring the burning in her head and the cramping in her leg--she raises the cup to his lips. She pours a little into his mouth, and he sputters and spits it out without waking. The second time she is more successful and he drinks a little, smacking and pursing his lips in displeasure.

Exhausted, Lien drinks a little more coffee and then returns to her prone position beside Fa. Her stomach burbles and she wonders whether their mysterious benefactor will provide them with food. She feels, at least, less afraid and more hopeful, with warm drink in her belly, and she drifts off into a dreamless sleep.

When she wakes again she is cold. The fire has died down to mere coals, and a fierce breeze has entered the cavern and spoiled their warm hideaway, carrying with it a flurry of snow.

Lien thinks she hears voices and sits up, crying out wordlessly and then shouting, "Here! We're in here!" Her head feels as if it will split in two, so she collapses back to the dirt and remains silent until the voices are louder and she can be sure she isn't imagining the sound. She calls again, and this time she receives a faint reply.

"Li? Li?"

Is that...Bao?! She sits up again and calls to him, then has to stop because the pain in her head is unbearable. Darkness threatens to take her into unconsciousness again but she won't let it, not so close to rescue.

Finally the voices are nearby, and she hears Bao saying, "Li? Li, is that you? You're alive!" He appears beside her, his face suffused with joy, his smile wider than she has ever seen it.

"And Fa, too," says another familiar voice: foreman Storbridge, whose lumbering bulk appears behind Bao, looking down disapprovingly at the injured workers. Several other Chinese workers gather around him. They're all wearing heavy furs and boots, and some carry lanterns and climbing ropes.

"I'm alive; someone's been taking care of us," Lien tells Bao. Tears stream from her eyes and down the sides of her face to pool in her ears. "They made us a fire and put splints on our broken bones. And there was coffee." She casts about for the copper tea kettle with its matching cup, but both are gone.

Bao's expression is worried as he looks at her broken leg. "Who did this?"

"I don't know," Lien says. She starts to shake her head but has to stop because of the pain. "I only remember a pale man. I must have been feverish; I don't remember much."

"It's good work," he confesses. "This stranger saved your life." Then he sighs and turns to her with earnestness sparkling in his black eyes. "I have to tell you, we thought you were dead. We came down here to look for a tunnel and collect your bodies."

"But we're not dead," Lien declares.

"And it's truly a miracle!"

Storbridge says something gruffly to Bao, so low and rapid Lien doesn't understand with her limited English. Bao replies; Storbridge walks away with a curt nod.

"We're going to set up camp here and explore these caverns," Bao explains. He gets up and goes to check on Fa, who remains unconscious, then returns to Lien. "I wish we knew who was taking care of you."

"I'm sure he'll return. He has to," Lien offers. Her stomach growls loudly and she laughs. "Until then, do you have some food?"

The workers are experienced in setting up camp rapidly, and tents are erected, the fire stoked to a healthy blaze, and tea kettles set to whistling within the hour. Both Lien and Fa are fed, though Fa is still unconscious and is given primarily tea. Lien devours dried fish and fruit from Bao's rations and gulps down hot tea while it's still boiling.

The Chinese workers sit near their injured

brethren and listen to Lien describe the pale man who has cared for her wounds. When she describes how she couldn't focus on his face and make out his features they start murmuring, and she hears the whispered word "demon".

"Stop being foolish," Bao chides the men. "We owe a debt of gratitude to this mysterious stranger, not whispered accusations."

"He saved my life," Lien confirms.

But when the stranger doesn't return that evening, the murmurs grow, and Lien catches suspicious glances being thrown her direction. She asks Bao to sleep beside her that night. "I don't trust the others."

"They're superstitious because this is all so mysterious. We really weren't expecting to find you alive."

Something about his guilty expression makes Lien ask, "Exactly how long have we been down here?"

Bao swallows. "Three days. That fall should have killed you, Li."

Lien's stomach churns. She thinks of the superstitious stories her parents told her as a girl, about demons and ghosts, and mutters a quick prayer to the ancestors. "Can we set up a shrine?" she asks.

"That's a good idea. The others will be comforted by a shrine as well. We don't have incense but we can make do." Bao goes to tell the others, and they begin to construct a small, makeshift shrine with the items available in their packs and in the cave. They build it closest to Fa, who clearly needs the most help from the ancestors. Soon small offerings of dried rations and tea are sitting before a chalk outline of the characters meaning "noble ancestors."

With Bao's help, Lien gets up and limps to the shrine, where she says a prayer and lays an offering of dried fish. She doesn't feel different as she returns to her position near the fire, but at least the other workers aren't glaring at her anymore. Her conscience a little clearer, she is able to sleep, though her leg throbs mightily after the movement and wakes her many times during the night.

Once she wakes and swears she sees movement near the shrine. She sits up and squints to see a figure hovering over Fa. She calls out to the figure and it turns and disappears into the darkness. Beside her Bao is deep in slumber, undisturbed by the noise, so Lien assumes she must be dreaming and lies down again.

The second time she wakes something prods her broken leg and the pain rouses her. She looks down to see a hulking figure crouched by her leg: Storbridge, barely visible in the dying firelight.

"Stop that!" she cries out, and tries to pull away from him; she gasps with pain as she tries to move the throbbing limb.

Storbridge turns and regards her with his eyes

narrowed in suspicion. There is something dark and menacing about him, and she doesn't like the way he looks at her, rather like a cat observing a bird with a broken wing. Lien reaches for Bao, but finds to her horror that his cot is empty.

"Your friend went to answer nature's call," Storbridge says, and though she doesn't understand all the words Lien comprehends that Bao has stepped away, leaving her unprotected.

"Leave me alone," she warns him. She's trying to sound intimidating but instead she sounds mewling and womanish.

The huge foreman tilts his head and regards her with increased interest. "There's something not right about you," he says softly, absently, speaking more to himself than to her.

"Go away," Lien says, her voice trembling. She looks about for help; the other Chinese workers are safely in their tent, far from the fire, and Fa remains unconscious beside the shrine.

Was that movement she saw in the shadows behind the shrine?

"Help me!" Lien calls out in English. This time her voice definitely gives her away; she has dropped all pretense and sounds like the woman she is.

Storbridge looms over her. With shocking alacrity he reaches down and tears at the blanket covering her.

Lien screams as he rips open her tunic to reveal her chest; she tries to cover her small breasts with her arms but her lie has been undone, the truth of her sex as obvious as her Chinese heritage.

Storbridge guffaws once, but then his shock turns rapidly to disbelief as he remembers that Lien is a member of his crew, and then rage as he recalls how quickly and skillfully the Chinese workers blast new tunnels and lay new rails, putting his white workmen to shame. And here, all along, there was a woman hiding among them. Maybe there are others; maybe the little yellow men have made a fool of him all along.

Lien screams as the foreman rushes her with a growl. The fire suddenly dies and engulfs the cavern in blackness.

Lien covers her face, expecting to be beset at any moment, but she remains miraculously unmolested. Slowly she uncovers her eyes and looks about; she can see nothing in the total darkness, but she can hear sounds of combat: the smack of fists on flesh and the thud of someone heavy hitting the ground, the soft "oof" of someone being punched in the gut.

Then she hears Bao's footsteps, unmistakable to her after their months together and her growing infatuation. "Bao! Help me!"

Bao rushes over to her, his hands seeking her in the dark. She reaches for him and they embrace clumsily.

When the fire flares to life again they both look down to see that her bare breasts remain exposed, pressed against his chest, and she quickly pulls the torn tunic closed over them.

"You're...you're....a woman!" Bao stutters, backing away from her.

Lien won't look at him. She clutches the tunic closed. "I thought you knew. *Xiong* figured it out."

Bao looks down to see the foreman beside him, on the ground, so bruised and battered that his face is barely recognizable. One of his arms hangs limp from the socket, twisted underneath his torso at an unnatural angle.

"What happened?" Bao demands.

"You really think I could do that? To *Xiong*?"

Bao looks at the man on the ground—who groans softly, and gurgles some blood onto the cave floor—and shakes his head. "I don't know. You're... you're..."

"Female, but not a demon—not strong enough to do *that*." Lien gestures to the crumpled body of the foreman. Tears sting her eyes. "After all this time together, you really think I'm capable of that?"

Bao starts to say something in retort, but the other workers come rushing out of the tent just then, pulling on their boots, stalling his words. The men rush over to the foreman, taking in the scene with expressions of shock and horror, and then glance at Lien. The tableau of her sitting helpless on her cot tells them a story. She holds her shirt closed with shaking hands, her face averted in shame.

The men all look to Bao, their eyes seeking. Lien knows Bao holds her future in his rough brown hands; with a word, he can condemn her or save her. Finally, without looking at her again, he sighs and says, "Help me," and lifts the foreman's ankles.

"What are you doing?" Lien demands as the workers gather up Storbridge and begin shuffling toward the cave entrance.

"If he lives, you'll never be safe again, Li—if that is your name," Bao says.

When the men return from dumping Storbridge's body in the snow, the others go to their cots in the tent and Bao feeds the fire. He makes sure Fa has slept through the adventure, and then he returns to sit beside Lien, in a meditative pose, saying nothing.

"Lien," she says softly.

He looks at her, his eyes searching her face for the truth.

"My real name is Lien," she repeats. "My parents called me Li and pretended I was a boy because I was their only child. I left to get away from them but I don't know how to be a woman, so I stayed Li even when I came over the ocean."

"Did you kill *Xiong*?" Bao asks.

"No."

"Then who did?"

"I don't know." Lien begins sobbing uncontrollably. Her careful house of lies has been demolished, and without her secrets she feels exposed and afraid. And now her closest friend, the man she thinks she might love, can't trust her, and believes she committed murder. "He attacked me," she tries to explain.

To her surprise, Bao places a hand on her knee. "I believe you. But if you didn't kill him, who did?"

"He's dead?"

Bao nods. "His neck was broken. He died while we carried him outside. Unless you truly are a demon, you don't have the strength to kill a man like that, so I believe you, because even if you aren't the man you claimed to be, I can't believe you're a demon."

Lien hugs him in relief, tears flowing even more freely now. "I don't know...what happened...the fire died..." she says through sobbing hiccoughs.

Bao lets her cling to him. "Did you see what happened?"

She shakes her head against his chest.

"The white men say this place is haunted."

Lien looks up at him, her huge, dark eyes reflecting the firelight. "They do?"

"A lot of the white men didn't want to come here. About twenty years ago some settlers moving west were trapped in this valley during the winter. They all died. The survivors...they ate their dead. They're cursed people now, and Donner Valley is cursed by their memory."

Lien shudders, remembering the women and children huddled around the tiny fire. Were these the victims of the hungry, wives and children devoured by their fathers and husbands?

"How horrible," she whispers, her dreams taking on sudden dark import.

Bao holds her close and strokes her hair. "But not all ghosts are evil," he says, staring out into the dark of the cavern, unafraid. "Some are just waiting."

*

The sun rises to find the group of Chinese rail workers already on foot, making their way slowly up the ravine to the mountain. The small group of eight men takes turns carrying the two invalids, both of them fortunately small and hardly burdensome. In the evening they make camp on a rocky promontory overlooking the valley, and one of them, the smallest, who has a broken leg, limps out of the tent at sunset to watch the glorious colors retreating in the sky as night settles over the ravine.

The others now know Lien's secret, but they've

sworn to keep it as best they can. She knows it won't remain secret for much longer—if Shen finds out, word will be all over camp faster than a swallow flies. As she watches the sunset, she thinks with dread of returning to the camp and lying about the fate of Storbridge. But what is the truth? What difference does it make whether he fell from a cliff wall or was pummeled to death by ghostly hands?

When darkness slides across the landscape, she retreats to her cot in the tent beside the other men. They sit in awkward silence, unsure how to behave now that her secret has been laid bare. She asks them to leave a lamp lit when they sleep; the darkness is unbearable for her now. She swears she can hear Storbridge breathing huskily, or the soft murmurings of the pale doctor who bandaged her wounds. Even years later, married to foreman Bao and mother to his children, she will not sleep without a lantern's glow or a stoked fire. She does not want to dream of the faceless bonneted women and their starving children, or remember the frozen nights spent in that strange cavern.

But, when the winter nights are bone-numbingly cold, her healed leg aches with remembered pain and her dreams are dark and haunted.

The Smoking Nun

When you arrive on my doorstep, your face will be haggard, dark circles pooling beneath your eyes. I'll open the door and you'll reel back as billows of acrid smoke pour into the alley. Then, squinting, you'll waft the smoke with one hand and try to see me in the sliver of doorway.

"Are you Chanda?" you'll ask, glancing furtively down the alley, examining every shadow.

I'll reach out and tap the sign that hangs beside the door. *The Smoking Nun*, it says, in four different languages. *Herbalist, occultist, psychic.* There's even a little painting of me, grinning and wreathed in smoke. I like that picture; it makes me look like a benevolent grandmother.

"I need your help," you'll say.

I'll nod and beckon you inside. You'll start coughing as soon as the door is closed, overwhelmed by the smoke. I'll guide you to a seat you can barely see and pour you a cup of tea so hot it steams.

"Drink it," I'll command in a voice that sounds like I'm either a heavy smoker or a creature that crawled out of the darkest depths of the sea. "Helps with the smoke."

You'll pick up the cup and cradle it in your hands, letting its warmth seep into your skin. You might blow on the liquid for a few seconds before taking a tentative sip. It will be bitter, it's always bitter, and you'll make a face. I'll laugh, with a sound like a drowning man's last desperate gurgle.

"What kind of nun are you?" you'll ask, glancing at the unfamiliar religious icons that crowd every surface of my basement apartment. You'll eye my saffron robes, brow furrowed.

I'll wave the question away. "You've never heard of it."

"I'm desperate," you'll finally say as I fumble with the hookah. "I've been to see priests, rabbis, ministers, even the pagan lady who sells tarot cards. No one can help me."

You'll pause, and when I gesture to continue the rest of the words will tumble out. "There's a creature following me. I think it's made of shadows. I know that sounds crazy, but I can see it moving in the darkness. My cat has disappeared. I sleep with the lights on now—but of course, I don't really sleep, not anymore." You'll give a nervous laugh. "It's not a demon or a golem or an evil spirit…."

"It's a harbinger," I'll rasp.

"Harbinger…of what?"

"Do you know what a deva is?"

Your eyebrows will draw together in an almost comical expression that is so predictable, I won't be able to stop myself from laughing again. "No."

"It's the Hindu word for deity. God."

"What does that have to do with me?"

I'll smile and offer you the hookah's mouthpiece. You'll hold up a hand to pass. "If you want my help, you'll smoke," I'll say.

You'll swallow, and frown, and maybe open your mouth to protest, but in the end your desperation will rule you. It's just one drag, what harm can it do? You'll close your lips around the mouthpiece and suck the smoke into your lungs. I'll do my best to remember what that first taste feels like, the surprisingly sweet flavor of the smoke on my tongue, the lightness spreading through my limbs as the herbs take effect.

"Seeing a harbinger means you're destined for greatness," I'll explain as I get up and make the remaining preparations. You'll stare at your numb fingers and your pupils will swell. If you're really lucky, your mouth will fall open and drool will drip down your chin. Meanwhile, I'll draw circles and lines in chalk on the floor around the table. I have the patterns memorized after so many years, but the lines are probably still mostly intact from the last time, so I'll need only to trace.

"I don't understand," you'll mumble, shaking

your head.

"Don't worry," I'll say, drawing the last few symbols and rising with a groan. My bones are getting old. "This will all be over soon."

You'll stare at me, and you'll notice the chalk in my hand, the dust on my skirt, and your eyes will go to the symbols on the floor. "What is this?" you'll gasp.

But now it's too late, of course. If you've retained enough motor control to attempt escape, you'll rise and stumble to the edge of the circle only to find that you can't leave. Most likely you'll be too high to stand, though. The herbs are twice as powerful when they've been consumed as drink and smoke.

At the end, as I stand over you and begin chanting, you'll mumble something pathetic, like "You were supposed to help me," or, my favorite, "Please, god, no." Ah, irony. Gets me every time.

Each deva is a unique experience. Your energy will taste like absinthe or honey or maybe rosewater. Don't worry, it doesn't hurt much; nobody screams or thrashes anymore thanks to the herbs. You'll feel very heavy and tired, fall asleep, and never wake again.

Well, not as yourself, anyway. Nothing will remain but shadow, a creature that seeks out slumbering gods. You'll try to warn them but—and this is my favorite part—you'll drive them right into my waiting arms, so desperate they'll drink my tea and smoke my hookah with barely any convincing required.

Once I'm sated, and you're reduced to a shade, I'll close all the curtains and return to my original form to bask in your divinity. If you're truly powerful, it might be days or weeks or even months before I emerge from my cocoon.

I love this country. It's like a buffet for someone like me, a place where people with divine blood can flee those who hunt them, a place where DNA is endlessly combined and recombined to create new gods from no familiar pantheon. *Give me your tired, your poor, your huddled masses yearning to be free.* For I am hungry. Very hungry.

When The Stars Are Right

After flying for nearly twenty-four hours, I shuffled out of the single-engine plane unsure of the time, the day, or my location. I'm not sure I could have even told you my name, and it's a miracle my lone bag was still clutched in my pale, clammy hand. I patted my pocket, finding comfort in the soft sound of paper crumpling, reassuring me the letter I'd carried thousands of miles had not been lost.

Cyrillic script slouched across the tower of the airport. A young man stood on the tarmac.

"I'm Arthur Goode," I croaked, my throat dry. "Are you my guide?"

The stranger nodded, smiling without showing his teeth. He was nearly a full head shorter than I, with dark hair and warm brown skin. His square jaw and high cheekbones made him effortlessly handsome, but his most striking feature was the amber-gold color of his eyes. They were the eyes of an otherworldly creature in a human face.

"Welcome to Zabroshennyy, Mr. Goode," he said in lilting English, all rolling r's and vowels so rich they practically dripped. "I'm Stepan Smirnov."

"Please, call me Arthur. Or...Artur, I suppose."

Stepan's smile broadened and his posture relaxed. "Glad to meet you, Artur." He reached over with familiar ease and pried my fingers from the handle of my suitcase. I groaned, my fingers stiff from clutching the bag in my lap for several terrifying hours. Stepan hefted the bag and gestured for me to follow him, taking off toward the parking lot at a trot. His quick, strong young body made me feel sad and jealous and warm with desire all at once. He led me to a silver sedan parked in front of the airport in a space that was definitely not legal.

My guide looked pleased when I elected to sit in the front passenger seat instead of the back. "So, what part of America are you from?" He turned the key in the ignition and the engine hummed to life.

I struggled to buckle my seatbelt with aching fingers. "Michigan. What part of Russia are you from?"

"Moscow! But I went to boarding school in England; that's why I speak very good English." The car leapt away from the curb and charged onto the street. I was surprised to see quite a bit of traffic zipping about the road. Zabroshennyy was not as small a town as I'd expected, despite its location far north of any major city and the tiny size of its airport.

"You probably speak better English than I do, if you were educated in the motherland." I gripped my seatbelt to keep myself from pawing at the dashboard.

"Ha! Motherland. I like that." The car swerved around a truck. Stepan twisted the wheel sharply to avoid another sedan. I gasped and clutched at my seat in a very undignified fashion. Stepan chortled with amusement and reached over to pat my knee tenderly. Was it my imagination, or did his hand linger on my leg just a moment longer than necessary? "Driving in Russia is very different from driving in America, but I've been doing it for years. You just leave it to Stepan."

I didn't really have much of a choice but to leave it to Stepan. I closed my eyes and forced my clenched muscles to relax, letting out a long, slow breath. When I opened my eyes, the edges of my vision were fuzzy. Pulling off my glasses, I squeezed my eyes shut again and pinched the bridge of my nose.

"Are you alright, Artur?" Stepan's words were like broken glass being shoved in my ears.

"I'm getting a migraine. I must've forgotten to take my medicine on the plane, with the time-change." My skull was full of pressure and my eyeballs wanted to explode from their sockets.

"Where is this medicine?"

"My bag, in the backseat."

I expected to feel the car braking and pulling onto the curb, but instead I felt Stepan's hand snaking into the backseat to grab the bag while the car continued to hurtle down the freeway. He pulled the bag between the seats and dropped it in my lap. I heard the zipper open and the rustle of his hand digging through the bag's contents, and then, finally, the sweet chime of pills clacking in a plastic bottle.

"How many?" he asked.

"Just one." I held up my palm and he dropped a single pill onto it. He folded my fingers over the capsule, the gesture once again considerate, tender, the press of skin becoming a soft brush as he released my hand.

The car jerked and swerved. Stepan shouted something in Russian and a car horn blared.

"Here," Stepan said, and I felt the smooth, rounded plastic of a water bottle against my fingers.

I tossed the pill into my mouth and followed it with a gulp from the water bottle. I was expecting lukewarm tap water, in all its slightly metallic, inoffensive glory, but instead I got a mouthful of something vile. It burned its way down my throat as I swallowed reflexively.

"What was that?" I demanded, opening my eyes to inspect the bottle. The contents were clear, a little too clear for water.

Stepan laughed and grinned. He clapped me on the back and then snatched the bottle from me to take a swig. "Welcome to Russia, my friend!"

One of the better side effects of the migraine meds is drowsiness. Once they were combined with the constant growl of the engine and the gentle rocking motion of the moving car, I found myself in a dozing state, sort of half-awake and half-asleep for hours. As usual, I dreamed of nightmarish landscapes, twisted trees with screaming faces, a bloody sky that boiled and oozed, and familiar black creatures dancing around a pink spire. Their sleek bodies shifted and oscillated, boneless arm-like appendages waving and thrashing. Their feet pounded a timpani drumbeat in my ears as lightning arced above, illuminating the scene in grotesque, oily light, casting shadows that called my name in thick, wretched voices.

I jerked awake to find myself wrapped in a blanket. The road before us was swathed in twilight; Zabroshennyy was somewhere behind us. The radio played softly and Stepan hummed along to a hair-metal ballad, something I recognized but couldn't name.

"Good morning, sleeping beauty." Stepan smiled down at me. "We're about an hour from our lodging."

"Do you need me to drive?" I rubbed sleep from my eyes.

Stepan shrugged. "If you drive, what do I get paid for? I like driving, anyway. How is your head?"

"Much better, thank you." My skull felt empty, like it would whistle if someone blew in my ear.

"Those pills knocked you right out. I'll need to get some of those for my next party. You were talking in your sleep, you know."

I felt myself turn red. "I do that sometimes."

Stepan's mien became serious. "It wasn't in English though."

I shivered, remembering the shadowy forms chanting in their oozing voices. "In Russian?"

Stepan shook his head. "I speak four languages and it wasn't one of the ones I know."

"You speak four languages?"

The serious moment was shattered by Stepan's hearty bark of laughter. "Don't sound so surprised! English, Russian, French and German. I would like to speak more but who has time for learning when there are Americans to schlep around, eh?" He grinned at me again, all white teeth and good humor.

My fear of the dream-creatures melted away under Stepan's huge, friendly grin and warm, golden gaze. My heartbeat quickened and I looked out the window. "I'm not so talented with languages; I only speak English. Mathematics are more my speed."

"And I can barely add two and two! Together we are the perfect team."

I had to laugh at that. "I guess we could be."

An hour later we pulled into the driveway of a lodge built in the log cabin style. Stepan unloaded our suitcases and carried them to our rooms. My bedroom featured a four-poster bed and a large bathroom with marble countertops and a shower big enough for four people.

Stepan introduced me to the lodge's matron, a small woman with silver hair and a quick, nervous smile. She made us an adequate dinner--spaghetti and meatballs, because the agency had told her an American was coming--and then, after showing Stepan where the booze was stored, retired to her own cabin.

"There's a hot tub, you know," Stepan said, grabbing a bottle of vodka and two glasses.

"I'm afraid I didn't bring any swim trunks," I replied.

He leveled me with a playfully stern look. "Why would you need swim trunks? It's a Tuesday. We're the only people here. You think Mrs. Ivanov is going to be offended? Please. She's on her fourth husband." Stepan marched out the lodge's back door and down the stone steps to the hot tub.

I watched from the window as he placed the bottle and glasses by the square shape in the ground, and then folded back the metal cover to reveal the largest whirlpool I'd ever seen. It would have fit at least twenty people, and was lit from within by lights that changed from blue to green. It looked like a mermaid's underground grotto.

Stepan stripped off his clothes in seconds. His naked body was only slightly paler than his arms, legs and face, still a warm, tawny brown. He had a firm, round ass. Retrieving the vodka, he turned so that he was facing the window, showing off all his goods, and waved at me with his free hand.

Heat rushed up my neck to my face. I gaped at him as he turned and climbed into the hot tub, all inhibitions apparently shed with his clothes. Or maybe Stepan had never possessed inhibitions at all.

I remembered the touch of Stepan's hand on my knee, his fingers closing over mine, the radiance of the smile he kept turning to me in the car. Was I reading too much into this? Was he just a flirt? We had two more days in a car together to look forward to, and that could get really awkward if I were misreading his intentions.

But I hadn't had a night of fun, the kind where I really relaxed and enjoyed another person's company, in a long time. Too busy with math and migraines. But what else was there to do out here in the Russian countryside, two days' drive from our destination?

A few minutes later I shed my clothes under Stepan's unflinching stare and joined him with a bottle of bordeaux I'd found at the back of the bar. The air was cold but the whirlpool was hot and delightfully bubbly.

"Vodka not good enough for you?" Stepan teased.

I poured wine into the glass he offered me. "I prefer wine, I'm afraid."

Stepan splashed water at me. "Are you sure you're

Russian?"

"That's what my birth certificate says, otherwise I wouldn't be here."

"Artur from Triska."

I swallowed a huge gulp of bordeaux. The wine tingled its way down my throat and into my stomach, where its effects spread to my limbs, hurried by the hot water, filling me with languorous lightness. I relaxed into the water, letting go of my self-conscious concerns about being too old, too pale, and too skinny for the gorgeous young man who shared the water with me. I leaned back and gazed up at the dark sky twinkling with stars.

"What do you hope to find when you arrive in Triska?" Stepan asked.

"My birth parents. You know that."

Stepan nodded and put aside his glass to drink directly from the vodka bottle. "But what do you *really* hope to find?"

I blinked at him, and then became very absorbed in my wine glass. I took a few more sips, letting the wine work its magic on my inhibitions, before I spoke. "The migraines are debilitating, and the doctors don't know what causes them, and can't stop them. I've never met anyone who has them like I do. I can't work, I can't maintain relationships, I can't do anything because I spend so much of my day either in agony or asleep. I spent the last of my savings to come here in the hopes that someone will be able to help me. Maybe I can find a kindred spirit, or some family lore will help me find a cure."

Stepan narrowed his eyes at me. "You're hoping for a miracle."

"Yes. A miracle. I know it's a longshot but I'm desperate."

He said nothing for a few long moments, and I felt the heat of an embarrassed blush creeping its way up my face. The hot water was suddenly boiling, and dizziness started to overtake me as my blood pressure rose. I placed my glass on the edge of the hot tub and moved for the stairs. "This was a mistake," I mumbled.

Stepan moved quick as a snake across the water and his hand closed around mine. His grip was strong and so sure, so certain, that I turned to him, startled. His face was very close, those yellow-gold eyes gazing into mine with a combination of compassion and lust with a twinkle of mischief.

A sob hitched in my throat and he kissed me. His lips were flavored like the sweet aftertaste of vodka.

Stepan called to me from high atop the gleaming pink glass spire that always haunted my dreams. Below him the dark creatures undulated and hissed. The air was acrid, thick with black smoke, choking me. Stepan and the glass spire were obscured by that smoke until all that

remained were his eyes, glowing like baleful yellow twin
suns.

I woke sputtering and coughing, choking
on my own phlegm. Sitting up, I gasped for air, my
heart thundering so hard the blood pounded a painful
drumbeat in my ears. Beside me, Stepan lay sprawled
across his bed. I touched his hair, comforting myself that
he was actually beside me, and very real. Eventually, my
heartbeat slowing, I slipped from the bed and crept out
of Stepan's room and back to my own.

For many long minutes I sat on the edge of my
empty bed and trembled. Then I fetched myself water
from the bathroom tap--it smelled like rotten eggs but
tasted only faintly of sulfur--and downed a pill. I curled
up on the mattress and willed myself to sleep so deeply
I wouldn't dream of the strange landscapes and illogical
monsters that usually assaulted my dreams.

Stepan's hand on my shoulder roused me. "Artur,
we should get on the road. It's nearly eight o'clock and
we have a long way to go."

I waved him off. "Tired. Let me sleep another
hour."

"Did I wear you out that much, old man?" His
lips tickled my ear. "Next time I'll have to be gentler."

I reached up and grabbed his hair, drawing his
face down to mine to kiss him. "Don't you dare."

He laughed with a throaty, sexy sound that made

my skin tingle. "You can sleep in the car if you need, I don't mind, but we have to go." As I slid from the bed, Stepan handed me a neatly folded stack of warm clothes. "We left them out by the hot tub overnight so I washed them and dried them."

"Oh god, Stepan...are you...are you a morning person?"

"You can hardly talk, you're an American! Besides, I made breakfast. There's even bacon. If you don't want it I can just leave it for Mrs. Ivanov..."

"No, no, I take it back." My stomach gurgled. "That's a compromise I can accept."

Breakfast was bacon, toast, and scrambled eggs. If I had any doubt that what happened the night before was a fluke or just a meaningless hookup, it was washed away under Stepan's attentions at the breakfast table. He barely nibbled at his food; he seemed to take more pleasure in watching me eat than he did in eating himself. He kept asking if I wanted another drink, salt or hot sauce for my eggs, more jam for my toast.

"You know I'm not going anywhere, right?" I asked.

He nodded and cleared our plates, pointedly not meeting my eyes. "Your return ticket doesn't take you home for another two weeks. I'm going to put the suitcases in the car."

I finished my breakfast and followed him,

wondering about that last remark.

Stepan liked to sing along to the radio, so we drove for some time listening to music. Lost in thought, I found myself pulling the letter from my pocket and smoothing it against my leg, my hand tracing the familiar folds in the paper.

"What's that?" Stepan asked.

"This? Oh. It's a letter from my mother, telling me I'm adopted."

"She told you by letter?" His voice was sharp with disapproval.

"She wrote it years ago but it was kept in a safe deposit box for a long time. We were estranged. My aunt sent it to me after my mom died last year." My index finger followed the ridge across the paper, swiping back and forth, back and forth.

"Estranged? I don't know that word."

"It means she disowned me and we didn't talk anymore. She didn't approve of my lifestyle."

"Ah. That I can understand. My mother wants me to get married and have babies with a fat Russian woman. I can't bear her disappointment, so we don't talk much anymore."

I didn't reply to that. It was a too-familiar tale that didn't bear relating all the details. Clumsily, I tried to change the subject. "That lodge was nicer than I was expecting. I don't suppose there's another on this route?"

Stepan shifted in his seat. "By tonight we'll be far from any lodges or hotels. Triska has been abandoned for many years, so there's not much in the surrounding countryside."

My stomach plummeted into my feet. "We won't be camping, will we?"

He chuckled. "I found a farmhouse where we can stay. We'll have to share a bed though. And last night..." he trailed off, his eyes shadowed with doubt.

I reached across the center console and laid my hand over his on the steering wheel. "I didn't stay in your bed last night because of the nightmares, Stepan. I didn't want to keep you awake all night."

Stepan smiled but it was tight, more like a quick pursing of his lips, and he wouldn't look at me, his eyes studying the road with unusual focus. I wracked my brain for something I could say to make him feel better, but exhaustion swept up over me and shadows encroached on the edges of the world. I pulled the pill bottle from my pocket and downed one dry. Snuggling into the blanket that smelled faintly of Stepan's cologne, I let sleep swallow me whole.

My dreams featured the usual surreal, terrible vistas, but the creatures that lurked in the darkest corners of my psyche drawled their hideous incantations in Russian. Their eyes were glowing amber orbs, their hands curled into menacing claws. They danced with impossible, unnatural gyrations beneath the pink spire, urging me to join their hellish frolic. They shrieked my name with Stepan's voice.

Flailing, I forced myself awake and found myself in a motionless car. Stepan sat beside me, his hands brushing the hair back from my face, calling my name in his gentle voice. I gulped air and groaned. A few tears burned their way from my eyes.

Stepan sighed. "I'm sorry I was angry, before. I understand now why you didn't want me to share your bed."

I reached up and gripped his wrist, meeting his eyes with mine. "It's better, now you're here. I don't have to wake up alone."

He smiled, his eyes like glittering like amber jewels, like shining golden coins. "I'm sorry you have such terrible dreams. Have you always had them?"

"My whole life," I admitted.

"What do you dream about?" He shook his head. "That was an insensitive question. I'm sorry."

"No, it's fine. It would be good to talk about it. I dream about...this pink tower. It's made of glass and it shines. At the base of it, there are these shadow monster things. They're drumming and dancing and chanting and it's very loud. Sometimes there's smoke, like car exhaust only thicker and burning the back of my throat."

"Every time the same dream?" Stepan's dark

brows drew together in concern.

I nodded.

"My babushka used to say that if you had a dream more than twice, it was bound to come true."

"What if you've had the same dream your whole life?"

Stepan didn't answer right away. Then he said, "I'm not sure my babushka really knew anything. I had that dream about my teeth falling out probably fifty times at university and they're still here."

I laughed. "And gorgeous."

He kissed me, a soft press of his lips against mine, then leaned back into his seat as if satisfied that I wasn't going to disappear if he moved away. "You were shouting in that language, you know. The one I don't recognize."

"What was I shouting?" I winced as I sat up. I'd scrunched way down in the passenger seat in my sleep and my back hurt with a dull pain that promised to be worse later. We were parked in front of a charming brick farmhouse. The sun had nearly set and the sky was navy, speckled with bright stars.

"I don't know. I told you, I don't speak that language."

"But what did I say? Do you remember the sounds?"

"What does it matter?" He frowned.

"I just...humor me, Stepan. Do you remember?"

Stepan's jaw clenched. "Yes, I remember. You were chanting it for half an hour before I woke you."

"Say it. I need to hear it."

He licked his lips and then, in a very low, very monotonous voice, he said, "Ph'nglui Mglw'nafh Nyarlathotep Triska wgah'nagl fhtagn."

A thrill of fear made every nerve ending in my body feel like it was on fire. "Are you sure?"

He narrowed his eyes at me. "Have you heard it before?"

"Yes," I gasped. "It's what the monsters say in my nightmare."

"What does it mean?"

A tear leaked from my eye and dripped down my cheek. "In his house in Triska dead Nyarlathotep waits dreaming."

"I thought you only spoke English."

"I do only speak English. I can't explain how I know what it means. I just do."

Stepan placed his hands on the steering wheel and leaned his forehead against them. "You don't want to go to Triska because of the migraines, do you?"

"No." Bile burned in my throat. "I'm sorry. I didn't mean to deceive you. I didn't know how to explain my reasons without sounding crazy."

Stepan lips became a thin, disapproving line, but then his tawny gaze flicked to me and he smiled sorrowfully. "I understand. I probably would've thought you were crazy. Who goes all the way to a village in Russia for a dream?"

I breathed a heavy sigh of relief. "Thank you for understanding."

"So who is this Nyarlathotep?"

The question caught me off guard. I looked down at my hands, studying the lines in my palms. I'd never discussed this with anyone before, except therapists who put me on increasing dosages of antipsychotics.

"No one knows. There's very little written about him. Some ancient god or another. But when I saw my Russian birth certificate and that I was born in a town called Triska...I thought, what if the dreams are memories? If I go back there, maybe I can remember. Maybe I can stop the dreams and, who knows? Maybe the migraines too."

"You think you're remembering a pink tower in the middle of the Russian tundra? With monsters dancing around it?"

I chortled, the sound harsh and grating in the quiet. "It sounds silly, when you put it like that. No, I think I'm misremembering. I was very young when I was adopted. I must've seen something when I was a baby that impressed itself onto my memory. The nightmares are me trying to make sense of it."

Stepan nodded, and then lifted his chin in the

direction of the road behind us. "We're only a few miles from Triska now. In the morning, you'll have your answers. But...Artur, I have to ask. Are you sure you want those answers?"

"What do you mean? Why wouldn't I?"

"Because whatever you saw when you were young was big and crazy enough to impress itself on a baby's memory."

The heat drained from my face. A ball of cold dread formed in my stomach, like a frozen stone.

"I know."

The farmhouse's owner was a swarthy man who eyed us with suspicion at first. He finally showed us to his spare room once Stepan handed him a thick wad of colorful Russian currency. He fed us beef stew and a dense, rye-like black bread for dinner, and then Stepan and I retired to our room. We played cards and drank vodka for an hour, laughing and making small talk, before eventually tumbling into bed. By unspoken accord, we bit back our sighs and moans, making love in silence so as not to disturb our host. Stepan tried his utmost to bring me to such heights of pleasure that I would break the quiet, but never succeeded.

We collapsed into a sweaty tangle of limbs in the wee hours of the morning. "Are you sure you don't want me to go sleep in the car? I thrash around pretty bad when I have nightmares," I warned.

Stepan held out his arms. "Do your worst, moy amerikanskiy."

"What does that mean?" I tucked myself in beside him.

He snorted, wrapping his arms around me. "You really are bad at languages. It means My American."

My heart clenched tight in my chest and I took a long, shuddering breath. "Your American?"

He nestled in against me, pressing the warm length of his body against mine. His breath stirred my hair and made me shiver as he whispered, "For as long as you want to be."

Sleep was like a velvet cloak wrapping around me, warm and soft, sucking me down into a dreamless stupor.

When I woke, Stepan was not in the bed beside me. I sat up and stretched. As the fog of sleep receded, I became aware the room wasn't as it had been the night before. The chair in the corner was tipped over; both the paintings that had been on the wall were now on the floor, frames cracked. I scowled at them, certain our lovemaking hadn't been *that* vigorous.

Then my eyes found Stepan's single shoe, upside-down beside the door, and somehow I knew he was gone. For a moment, I thought perhaps he'd left of his own volition, but then why would the room be ransacked?

And then I knew, with a hot lance of terror through my chest, that he'd been taken.

My gaze was drawn to something on the ceiling, a smear of rust-brown. It was a single word, the Cyrillic letters hastily painted, probably by fingers in the dark. The arrangement of the letters was familiar. Holding my breath, I found my jeans on the floor and pulled out the letter with my birth certificate still attached. I unfolded the certificate and held it up to compare the symbols written on the paper with the word painted on the ceiling:

Triska.

A sob tore its way from my mouth. I sat crying and gasping for a few moments, trying to comprehend what was happening. Stepan's clothes were still scattered around the floor. Someone had abducted him from my bed, naked and unarmed, and now they were trying to lure me to the town of my birth. I was going there anyway, so why would they take Stepan to force me there?

My first instinct was to contact the authorities for help. Without Stepan to translate for me, that would be difficult, but not impossible. I pulled on my jeans and rushed, barefoot and shirtless, downstairs to find our host.

The front door stood open, letting in a breeze that rose chill-bumps on my naked arms. An unmoving body lay draped across the threshold, face down on the floor, propping open the door. A pool of blood surrounded the body and I stopped my feet just in time to prevent myself from stepping in it. The smell of blood hit me and I vomited onto the floor beside the body, heaving so hard my eyes filled with stars.

As my vision cleared, I tried to piece together what had happened last night while I slept. The farmer had been killed by the same people who abducted Stepan, which meant I didn't have time to call for help. I needed to get to Triska.

I raced back upstairs and dressed, throwing both my clothes and Stepan's into our bags. Thankfully, the car keys were still in Stepan's pocket. I used the back door to escape the house instead of stepping over the farmer's corpse, trying not to look at the body as I snuck away, holding my breath to block out the smell.

My ears rang with a high-pitched whine and my vision narrowed to a bright tunnel while I threw our bags into the sedan's backseat and slid behind the wheel. Now was not the time for a migraine, but no doubt it had been brought on by stress. I took a few deep breaths, trying to calm myself, but my blood continued to beat in my ears.

I eyed my bag. I could take a pill and stop the freight train that was about to bear down on my brain. But then I wouldn't be able to drive myself to Triska. It would be risky enough, driving with a migraine dulling my senses, but it would be impossible if I was drugged. The thought of escaping this horror was tempting, but if I took a pill I would merely be dragging myself from the Hell of reality to the Hell of my nightmares, and I would doom Stepan in the process.

I pulled the map from the glovebox and charted the route to Triska.

Hours later, I spotted the squat industrial buildings of the abandoned town and wept with relief. They were painted in bright, friendly colors, but even from a distance I could tell the paint was faded and peeling. The road sign announcing Triska was rusted and overgrown with vines. Stray dogs dashed from the street as I drove into town.

My head felt like it was stuffed with angry hornets. The mountains in the distance pulsed with each beat of my heart, and the road writhed and lashed like the tail of an angry snake. The sun was too bright, the shadows too dark, the baying of dogs in the distance like knives to my eardrums.

As I drove through town, I looked for any sign of human habitation. I rolled the window down and called for Stepan, hoping he would hear my voice and respond. I was answered by howling dogs and cackling crows and my own voice reverberating off the abandoned buildings.

My head pounding, my hopes of finding Stepan sinking, I eventually abandoned the car to walk the streets, calling for Stepan in a voice becoming weaker and hoarser with each passing minute. The sun was already low on the horizon--it seemed too early for the mantle of evening to settle over the land, but I reminded myself that this was Russia. I was very far north, further than I'd ever been in my life.

Something flashed in my vision and I looked up to find the mountains gleaming pink and orange in the sunset. My breath caught. Was this the pink spire from my vision? The mountains wavered before me, my vision narrowing from a tunnel to a pinpoint. The migraine was finally taking my sight. I sank to my knees in the street. The breeze ruffled my hair, and somewhere nearby a dog yipped. I closed my eyes and put my head in my hands.

Stepan was lost to me. I would probably die here in Triska, ripped apart by wild dogs.

A strangled scream cut through the rushing of blood in my ears. I lifted my head and blinked my eyes, willing myself to see. My vision cleared for a few seconds, and then blacked out again. Applying all my willpower, I managed to see in spurts and starts. The pain was excruciating each time my vision returned, but I staggered to my feet and followed the scream, stumbling forward, running into walls and tripping over trash. The sky swirled with trails of every color and the buildings of

Triska glowed like brightly colored lanterns. The ground pulsed and trembled, throwing me to my knees again and again. Each time, the scream sounded, echoing off the abandoned buildings, and I wept and cursed but pulled myself to my feet and stumbled ever onward.

Stepan was tied in the town square, surrounded by people in long black cloaks with hoods. They chanted in low, monotonous voices, the sound just audible under Stepan's screams. One of them gripped a long knife and used it to score Stepan's chest with slow, agonizing strokes, leaving his flesh flayed and bloody. Above them, the sky was like boiling paint, glowing and scintillating with color.

I rushed forward, aiming to snatch the knife from the hand that tortured my lover, but my vision blinked in and out. The cultists closed around me, grabbing my arms and holding me back.

"Stepan!" I screamed, struggling weakly against the strong hands that gripped me.

"Artur," Stepan whimpered, and then he gasped and gurgled. My vision returned for a fraction of a second, just long enough to see the slash of red across his throat, his golden eyes rolling back as his lifeblood poured from the wound and down his flayed torso.

Rage and sorrow coursed through me. My senses filled with the sound of chanting, the smell of blood, the flickers and flashes of the colorful lights in the sky. And then my whole world was agony, like my brain was on fire. To cope with the pain, I disassociated and watched myself from above. Arthur Goode writhed and thrashed on the ground below me, surrounded by chanting cultists. And then his body began to change, to expand, to undulate and pulse like the lights in the sky. His arms elongated, his face melted, and his human skin peeled away like a molting spider's exoskeleton to reveal an infinite darkness.

I knew, then, what the cultists chanted. It was my name: Nyarlathotep.

With that knowledge came the knowledge of a thousand eons. I knew the names of every star and every dark god who resided upon them. I knew every name I'd been given for a million years, on a thousand worlds, and I knew where the edge of the universe unraveled into nothingness.

The cultists looked up at me with eyes glittering triumphantly, but all I could see was Stepan's tortured corpse. I opened my mouth and it became a void. Each of the cultists were sucked screaming into the darkness. Silence settled over the town square, the lights above us dimming as if recoiling from my terrible power.

With a gesture, I repaired Stepan's tormented flesh and released him from his bonds. With a thought, I drew his soul from the abyss and returned it to his body. His eyelids fluttered open and he gaped at me. I could see an amber-gold version of myself reflected in his eyes: the black hole of my mouth, the boneless motion of my limbs, the countless eyes that covered my inky flesh.

I shrank down to human size. "Now that you've seen my true form, will you run?"

Stepan eyed me cautiously. "Are you still Artur?"

"I am Nyarlathotep, He Of Many Eyes, The Crawling Chaos, The Outer God, trapped in human form for forty-six years in an attempt to prevent my inevitable supremacy."

He blinked and tears glittered in his eyes. "But are you still Artur?"

I rearranged myself into the shape of the human called Arthur Goode. "I am Arthur Goode, and so much more. So will you run? Or will you rule by my side, the beloved of this world's dark god?"

Stepan reached up and cupped my jaw with his warm hand.

"I would never leave you, moy amerikanskiy."

I enclosed Stepan in my embrace and breathed the scent of his skin. "Where shall we go, my beloved? All of time and space is our playground."

Stepan clasped my hand in his. "I've never been to America. I want to meet your family; I want to see where you were raised."

I chortled. "All of time and space, and you want to go to Michigan?"

Stepan grinned up at me, amber eyes flashing. "You heard me. Why are we still standing here, Mister all-powerful-outer-god? Let's go."

And we did.

Dead Girls Don't Love

I had no memories before Princess came along. Papa Levi put her on the cot next to mine one night and I lay in the darkness, wondering about the source of the intoxicating smell of lavender and honey that drifted across the expanse of floor between our cots. Of course, I couldn't compare the scent to anything then, my mind blank as an unwritten page.

The next day, when she came to work beside me in the field, I recognized her scent. I felt strange, as if my heart were clenching tight in my chest. It was the first time I'd remembered anything from one day to the next, aside from my name and how to dig a hole in the earth. And sometimes I forgot those too. Memories are hard to cling to when you're dead.

Princess's skin was a rich brown, the color of the earth we tilled. Her hair was cropped, like every other worker's, but it was such a dark brown it was nearly black. And her eyes were green, startling against her dark face, paler than the weeds we ripped from the earth bare-handed until our palms bled. She was beautiful.

"Hello," I said when Papa Levi left her beside me.

She blinked at me, squinting against the sunlight,

but didn't reply. This was a normal reaction for a new worker, so I didn't worry. Words would come to her eventually. Or they wouldn't. As long as she could do the work, the farm would keep her, either way.

We worked side-by-side tearing up weeds that day, and that night I lay awake on my cot, listening to her cry.

"Why?" I asked her, watching her in the dim moonlight that streamed in between the wall slats. She worked her jaw but still couldn't speak. I didn't know why she was upset, but I knew the sound she was making was a sound of sorrow. I wasn't allowed to get up from my cot, but I wanted to make her stop. So I stretched my arm across the dirt floor, seeking her hand.

She pulled away from me, rolling onto her other side and sniffling. I retracted my hand, wishing I could do more.

The next day Papa Levi put her beside me again. "This is Cupcake. Follow her lead." He gestured to me and pushed a trowel into her hand. She stood staring at the ground for a few long moments, then looked at me, stupid as a newborn.

"Like this," I said, reaching down and digging a little hole with my own trowel. I liked digging holes, I was good at it. I looked up at Princess. She was staring off into the distance, paying me no mind.

I stood and grabbed her wrist. Her eyes snapped

back to my face. "Like this," I told her, and gestured to the holes in the ground. She looked at the holes and looked at me, then at the trowel in her hand. I led her to a spot beside the hole I'd dug. "You try."

She squatted beside the hole and stuck her trowel in the earth. She didn't know what to do after that and looked at me. I knelt and placed my hand over hers.

The touch was like electricity. A tingling sensation spread from my hand to my heart. Our eyes locked. Time stopped.

"What're you two doin'?" A familiar voice boomed. "Cupcake? Princess?" Mama Tess glided up to us, the necklace of animal skulls she wore about her neck clacking. Her face was a twist of anger.

I stood and my trainee followed suit. "Diggin'," I said, gesturing to the half-dug hole in the earth.

Mama Tess's blow caught me off guard, as it always did. She struck me so hard I tasted blood. She drew her hand back for a second strike, but Princess was there. Her hand came up and caught Mama Tess's wrist.

"No!" I cried.

Princess turned to look at me, still holding Mama Tess's wrist. She looked confused, hurt, angry.

"No," I told her again, shaking my head. Princess slowly released the wrist.

Mama Tess called for Papa Levi while she rubbed her wrist. He came with the shovel and hit Princess on the back a few times to teach her a lesson. She didn't scream or cry out as the shovel came down, just whimpered and looked at me with eyes like a puppy's. Innocent, stupid, empty. She didn't understand why this was happening. She didn't understand why I didn't help her.

I couldn't help her. Not with Mama Tess and Papa Levi standing there. They couldn't kill me, since I was already dead, but they could bury me again. Being buried again was my worst fear. What if I couldn't dig my way out this time? I'd be trapped in the dark forever. Anything was better than that, even working from sunrise to sunset and watching a beautiful woman hit with a shovel until she stopped moving.

So I didn't help, and forced myself to feel nothing about it, not even regret. Emotions were for the living.

That night Princess didn't cry. She didn't speak. She just lay on her cot, a lump of human flesh, barely breathing. She still wouldn't take my hand, though I left it on the dirt between our cots all night.

The next day Papa Levi didn't put Princess beside me in the field. I dug holes and wondered where she was, what task she was doing. I had never thought about anything besides the work before. Without memories, what else was there to consider? My past was erased and my future was there, in that field—the present was all I had.

Until Princess. And then I wondered. I missed her scent. For the first time since I'd been brought to the farm, I felt something.

Regret. Guilt. Worry.

At supper I was relieved to find that Princess was doling out the grits. "Hello," I said, extending my bowl and smiling.

She ladled grits into my dish and didn't meet my eyes. I picked at my food and went to bed. I lay awake until Princess came to her cot.

"I'm sorry," I whispered when the lights went dark. I wasn't sure what the words meant, but they seemed right.

I heard her soft intake of breath. "Sorry?" she repeated.

"Sorry." My heart fluttered in my chest like a moth. She was speaking, and speaking to me!

"What is sorry?"

"I don't know," I admitted. Then I laughed, the sound too loud in the quiet barracks, and clapped my hand over my own mouth.

To my surprise, she laughed too, and we fell asleep whispering "I'm sorry" and "I don't know" back and forth, giggling like children and hiding the words behind grimy hands.

The next few days were full of forbidden glances over grits that would make me tingle. Princess became my every thought. Each time I dug a hole in the field I would lean down over it and whisper her name into the earth. I had no words to describe what I was feeling and no one to whom I could confess my sins. The other workers were mindless drones. When I spoke to them, they just stared, or replied with a simple "Hello." I wasn't sure whether they were really so stupid or whether they were too frightened to exchange words.

One afternoon Mama Tess came tromping across the field, a shotgun balanced on one shoulder, trailed by a house worker, a girl who looked like Princess. Not exactly like Princess, but enough. Her skin was lighter and her eyes were brown, but she wore the same cotton shift and she was just as pretty.

Her belly protruded, and I couldn't help but stare. What was wrong with her? The dead don't get sick.

Mama Tess took her to the apple orchard across the field from the house. I returned to scooping dirt over the seeds that had been placed in the holes I'd dug days before.

The shotgun blast was jarring. I looked up from the field, along with all the other workers. I saw the girl's silhouette slump to the ground among the apple trees. Mama Tess walked away, leaving the body where it had fallen.

Papa Levi passed me on his way to the orchard, carrying a burlap sack and a shovel.

"That's the last time I clean up yo' mess," Mama Tess growled as he passed her.

I stood in the field watching the living come and go and wondered. Why would Mama Tess shoot a dead person? Why not just bury her, as they always did, and let her reemerge from the soil if she was strong enough, or stay buried if she wasn't? I watched as Papa Levi bundled the buckshot-riddled corpse into his sack.

I looked out over the heads of the other workers, already returning to their labor, too stupid or scared to know what had happened. Too dumb and frightened to realize...

Realize what? Thoughts could only form halfway in my muddled mind. I stood staring, thinking, trying to make something of the jumbled mess in my head.

"What you doin', Cupcake?" Mama Tess, somewhere behind me. Her tone was accusatory.

I knelt and scooped dirt over a hole, but it was too late. Mama Tess had seen me pause. She boxed my ears so hard they rang. Then she kicked me, hard, so that I toppled over sideways and lay curled around my knees like a potato bug, trying to protect my face and body from her blows. She hit me with the rifle butt a few times, bruising my ribs, before Papa Levi stopped her.

They exchanged words in heated voices; I was in too much pain to hear anything more than a constant buzz.

Papa Levi slung me over his shoulder and carried me back to the barracks, dropping me on my cot. "Thinkin's for the living, Cupcake. You a dead girl now." His breath stank of whisky and rot. His eyes looked me up and down. He licked his lips, made a face like he was disgusted, and then hurried out of the barracks.

Later that night, I listened to Princess breathe in her sleep. The moon was dark, the barracks a lightless tomb. I thought about what had happened in the apple orchard, about the shotgun, about killing a walking corpse. I thought about dead people who eat and sleep and till fields. I thought about the mysterious bump under the dress of the house worker Mama Tess had shot. My thoughts were like an unraveling sweater: they led somewhere, but the more I tugged the less the shape of the thing made sense.

I did know one thing, though. I knew that Princess was in danger. The face of the girl in the orchard haunted me. She looked so much like Princess. I wondered if I could have saved her; I wondered if I could save Princess.

In the quiet darkness of the barracks, I could hear the living in the house a hundred yards away: the low rumble of Papa Levi's voice, the shrill wail of Mama Tess's laughter. Light flashed between the slats of the barrack walls, and I heard the front door of the house open and close with a slam. Then the sound of heavy, slow footsteps, growing louder. Eventually someone fiddled with the padlock, and the barracks door creaked open. The stench of whisky and rot curled my lip.

"Princess," Papa Levi whispered. When Princess didn't stir, he whispered again, louder. This time, her steady breathing stopped with a soft gasp, but she didn't move.

"Come 'ere, Princess," Papa Levi drawled. "Git up." He stumbled into the barracks. I couldn't see him in the dark, but I could hear him slapping the foot of each cot, counting his way to Princess's.

I grabbed Princess's arm and tugged. She rolled off her cot, across the floor and onto mine. I wrapped my arms around her. She trembled like a tree in a storm. I pressed my face against hers and squeezed my eyes shut tight, hoping that I could will us invisible.

"Where you at?" Papa Levi grunted, slapping at the empty cot with his huge hands. His breaths were loud and rasping. I held onto Princess and wondered whether a skinny dead girl could fight off a living man who had the advantage of both strength and size.

Mama Tess's scream cut through the quiet night. "LEVI! You best get yo' ass back up to this house afore I come lookin'!"

Sighing, Papa Levi stood and stumbled to the door. "I'm a-coming, woman." He staggered out of the barracks and back toward the house, his footsteps retreating.

He hadn't shut or locked the barracks door.

I leaped to my feet and pulled Princess up with me. I ran for the door, but Princess yanked her hand from my grip and returned to her cot.

"What?" I demanded.

"Sleepy."

"No! Princess. *Princess!* Come on." I grabbed at her arms.

She slapped me away. "Sleepy."

I could hear Mama Tess and Papa Levi on the porch of the big house, arguing. How long before one of them came to check that the door was locked? I had to get out while I could. I had to leave Princess. I made one more attempt to pull her from her cot, but she was too heavy for me to carry and let out a reluctant moan. The voices from the distant porch went quiet.

They'd heard us. I let go of Princess and ran.

The barracks were surrounded by fields. There was nowhere to hide, but the moon was gone from the sky and the landscape was dark enough that I could tear across the field toward the house without being seen. I waited just beyond the circle of bright electric light cast by the house's windows, watching as Mama Tess and Papa Levi made their way to the barracks.

Mama Tess started shrieking and I dashed for the porch.

I didn't have a plan. My brain was still too befuddled for that. I ran into the house, shielding my face from light that seemed unnaturally bright after so many months living without electricity. I followed each open door from room to room, the words for each coming back to me as I ran—kitchen, dining room, family room—until I found a door that was closed. I tried to turn the knob but found it locked. I slammed my weight against it uselessly, too skinny and weak to force my way in.

Mama Tess's shrieking was growing closer.

Panicking, I ran upstairs. The steps were strange to me at first. I didn't really know how to use them, and ran up with both hands and feet. But as I ascended I remembered, vaguely, how stairs worked. I knew I would find bedrooms on the second floor. I knew what bedrooms were. As soon as I tried to grasp the memories, they slid away, slippery as sweat-soaked skin, and I was left gasping at the top of the stairs.

The master bedroom was obvious. A huge four-poster bed dominated the room and the walls were papered in delicate pink roses. I grappled with memories of my own bedroom, somewhere, back when I'd been alive. One of Mama Tess's shapeless house dresses was draped across the bed. There was a bulge in one pocket.

I reached into the pocket and pulled out a key ring with four keys dangling from it.

Clutching the keys, I ran back downstairs. Papa Levi's voice bellowed through the house. "CUPCAKE! Whatever you doin', you best stop! Doing's for the livin'!"

Terrified, I fumbled the keys. My heart was beating so hard I could feel it hammering a staccato rhythm behind my rib cage. I breathed in ragged, desperate gasps, my lungs aching. My vision narrowed to a dark tunnel. I had to grip my shaking right hand with my left hand to force the first key into the lock. I tried to turn it, but it was the wrong key. I drew the key out to try another.

Papa Levi's shovel hit me hard across the shoulders, knocking me to the floor. The keys flew from my hands and away even as I reached for them. Papa Levi drew the shovel back for a second blow. I rolled away from him and the shovel came down on the floor with a *thwack*.

I scrambled to my feet and crouched, ready to fight or flee though my shoulders hurt with a burning, stabbing pain.

Papa Levi blinked at me. "How? You dead. You a *dead thing*!" He lunged at me, but he was drunk and I was fast. I ducked out of the way of his shovel and he brought it down on the furniture.

Mama Tess appeared in the doorway. "What is goin' on in here?" When she saw me, she screeched. "Cupcake! Levi, git her."

Again, I ducked Papa Levi's clumsy attack.
This time he threw himself off balance and the shovel
slipped from his hands, flying across the room. I ran for
the shovel and found the keys beside it. Raising both, I
backed toward the locked door.

"Cupcake! What're you doin', you stupid dead
thing?" Mama Tess called. "Levi, git the gun!" She
started toward me, her face puckered in fury and hands
outstretched as if she would squeeze my throat.

I drew back the shovel and swung at her. I was
weak from months of malnourishment and my shoulders
burned, but there was enough hate in me that the swing
was powerful anyway. I'll never forget the sound it made
as it crushed Mama Tess's head, like a *clang* and a *crunch*
all at once.

Papa Levi was going for the stairs, but heard the
sound and turned back. His eyes were wide. He staggered
over to Mama Tess and knelt beside her. A sound like
a dog's howl tore its way from his throat, a sound that
made my skin prickle. He lifted Mama Tess into his arms
and rocked her, throwing his head back to give volume to
that terrible keen.

I dropped the shovel and chose another key. My
hands were remarkably steady as I slipped the key into
the lock. The door swung open.

The room was filled with the bitter odor of
burning wax. On the far wall, an altar was covered in

213

melted candles, dried flowers, and scattered bones. The centerpiece was a statue of a slender man in a top hat, his face painted like a skull: Baron Samedi, God of Death.

The rest of the room was filled with shelves, and on every shelf there were jars and bottles. Dozens of them, maybe hundreds, all different sizes and shapes and colors. Some were just ordinary mason jars, others were soda bottles. Each jar contained what appeared to be a single firefly, a soft glow that flickered and danced.

I lifted the shovel and entered the room. For a moment I savored the beauty of the fireflies, the triumph of the moment.

"Cupcake?" Princess stood in the doorway. She looked like a sapling in a cotton dress.

She took a step, as if to come inside, but I held up a hand to stop her. "No," I said. I hefted the shovel. I turned and swung it, smashing the nearest jar. I swung again and again, smashing jar after jar. The sound of breaking glass became a symphony.

As the jars broke into thousands of shards, the glowing lights dissipated.

Memories came over me like a massive wave, drowning me and punching me and tossing me around like so much driftwood. Even as I was assailed by memories, I kept swinging the shovel, desperate to succeed in my mission, desperate to free every last worker from the senseless Hell we'd come to know. I couldn't see or hear, my vision obscured by faces that came rushing back, my hearing full of words and names and sounds I hadn't known I was missing.

I felt a hand on my arm. "Heather. Heather, stop. I think they're all smashed."

I opened my eyes and turned to see Princess, her face beside mine, her hand on my arm. I dropped the shovel. "Deja," I whispered.

She smiled, tears flooding her green eyes and escaping down her cheeks. "How did I forget your eyes?" I asked, taking her face in my hands and swiping at her tears with my thumbs.

Deja laughed. "I don't think you did forget." She pulled me into her arms and kissed me. Her lips were salty and soft. Months of depredations and trauma were swept away in that kiss. All the beatings and starvation were erased for a moment in my lover's arms. I remembered our first kiss at a movie theater, our engagement kiss beneath the spray of Niagara Falls, our wedding kiss in a sun-dappled clearing while our friends applauded. We kissed a thousand times when our lips met that night.

"Dead girls don't love." Papa Levi stood in the doorway, his fists clenched at his sides. "Dead girls don't *kiss*."

Deja and I separated. "We're not dead girls," she said, lifting the shovel and hefting it with both hands.

"We never were." I reached for a huge shard of glass and brandished it though the sharp edges bit into my palm.

Papa Levi sneered, all furrowed brow and bared teeth. Deja and I crouched, ready to spring when he made his move.

The front door slammed. Papa Levi looked away from us, toward the sound. Horror dawned on his face, and then he forgot all about the kissing girls in the jar room as he turned to flee instead. He was pursued by screaming workers, their wits returned to them, their filthy hands gripping whatever tools they'd been able to find in the fields. Their ululations were the cries of the vengeful, the tortured, the justified.

It was only then I realized Deja and I were standing barefoot in a room full of broken glass. We dropped our makeshift weapons, clasped hands, and started toward the door. I hesitated and looked back. The statue of Baron Samedi still grinned at me. "Wait," I told Deja.

Tiny pieces of glass dug into my feet as I returned to the room and picked up the shovel. With a triumphant cry, I brought the blade down on the baron's head, smashing the figurine into countless pieces of porcelain.

Wincing, I limped back to Deja. We made our way out of the house and down to the main road, our fingers laced tightly together. My injured shoulders burned and my sliced feet stung, but my heart was singing.

Behind us, the farm went up in flames, a yellow beacon in the darkness.

Sarah Hans is an award-winning writer, editor, and teacher. Sarah's short stories have appeared in over twenty publications, but she's best known for her multicultural steampunk anthology Steampunk World. You can read more of her short stories, nonfiction ramblings, and novel chapters on her Patreon for just $1/month at https://www.patreon.com/sarahhans or find her on twitter at https://twitter.com/steampunk-panda.

Dragon's Roost Press is the fever dream brainchild of dark speculative fiction author Michael Cieslak. Since 2014, their goal has been to find the best speculative fiction authors and share their work with the public. For more information about Dragon's Roost Press and their publications, please visit: http://thedragonsroost.net/styled-3/index.html.

The
Dragon's Roost Press

Also Available from Dragon's Roost Press by Sarah Hans

An Ideal Vessel

Not long ago, Zuzanna Uritski was a cleaner at the 1893 Chicago World's Fair, Archibald Campion was the Fair's most imaginative engineer, and Elspeth was a lifeless automaton.

But now? Now they're demon hunters, pursuing an ancient evil that has traveled across universes to take residence in one of history's most famous serial killers.

Travel to an alternate history where no one is safe from demon possession, automatons are self-aware, and the world's greatest hope lies with a clever engineer, a dauntless young woman, and a paladin from another world.

Also Available from Dragon's Roost Press
Hidden Menagerie Volumes 1 & 2

Edited by Michael Cieslak   Edited by Michael Cieslak

Welcome to the Hidden Menagerie -- a collection of short fiction involving various cryptozoological creatures. In the first volume you will meet the beasts of the land. Inside these pages you will be introduced to new visions of some creatures you are familiar with like the Abominable Snowman and the Wendigo, creatures long thought extinct which live on to this day, and others you may have never heard of.

In the second volume you will meet the beasts of the air, sea, and animate vegetation. Inside these pages you will be introduced to new visions of some creatures you are familiar with like the Kraken, Mermaids, and Lake Monsters, creatures long thought extinct which live on to this day, and others you may have never heard of. These volumes contains 35 stories by some of the best dark speculative fiction writers working today.

A portion of the proceeds from all sales of Hidden Menagerie Vols 1 & 2 benefits the Lost Day Dog Rescue Organization.

Also Available from Dragon's Roost Press

Robotic Animals
Televisions Which Reveal Alternate Universes
Inanimate Objects Brought to Life
People Struggling to Survive in Apocalyptic Wastelands
Sentient Cutlery

and much, much more

Desolation: 21 Tales for Tails is a collection of dark speculative fiction whose stories all focus on themes of loneliness, isolation, and abandonment.

Enter into strange worlds envisioned by some of the most inventive writing today.

Combine the mind splintering horror of the Cthulhu Mythos and the heart shattering portion of that most terrible of emotions -- love -- and what do you have? You have *Eldritch Embraces: Putting the Love Back in Lovecraft*.

Some of the best authors working in the fields of horror and dark speculative fiction blends romance and Lovecraft in a way which will make you sigh, smile, weep, or leave you the hollow shell of your former self.

Also Available from Dragon's Roost Press

Hidden Menagerie Volumes 1 & 2

Edited by Michael Cieslak

Edited by Michael Cieslak

Welcome to the Hidden Menagerie -- a collection of short fiction involving various cryptozoological creatures. In the first volume you will meet the beasts of the land. Inside these pages you will be introduced to new visions of some creatures you are familiar with like the Abominable Snowman and the Wendigo, creatures long thought extinct which live on to this day, and others you may have never heard of.

In the second volume you will meet the beasts of the air, sea, and animate vegetation. Inside these pages you will be introduced to new visions of some creatures you are familiar with like the Kraken, Mermaids, and Lake Monsters, among others. These volumes contain 35 stories by some of the best dark speculative fiction writers working today.

A portion of the proceeds from all sales of *Hidden Menagerie Vols 1 & 2* benefits the Lost Day Dog Rescue Organization.

Also Available from Dragon's Roost Press

Jericho Rising

by Mary Lynne Gibbs

In post-World War III, small town Michigan, a self-proclaimed, violent, and insane High Priestess has taken control, reducing the remaining men to nothing more than slaves and playthings.

Jericho, the reluctant leader of the Resistance, must fight her own family to preserve the freedom and equality of all in her care – male and female alike. She's torn between love and duty, and with traitors around every corner, she has no idea who to trust anymore.

Also Available from Dragon's Roost Press

Jericho's Redemption

by Mary Lynne Gibbs

The battle is over, but the war has just begun. Jericho returns to the Obsidian camp, only to learn that her sister Candace destroyed it as part of a plot to dismantle the resistance movement that brought down their mother, the High Priestess. The rest of the resistance blames Jericho for the deaths of their friends, but that's the least of her worries. Not only does Jericho now have to right the wrongs her sister has done, she must contend with a few guests to the camp who bring secrets that will change her life forever. Either she'll redeem herself in the eyes of her comrades, or she'll die trying.

Also Available from Dragon's Roost Press

 **The Maiden's Courage**

by Mary Lynne Gibbs

The best man on the pirate ship is a girl named Alex.

Alexandra "Alex" Gardner is the reluctant cabin boy on *The Bloody Maiden*, a ruthless pirate ship run by the charmingly evil Captain Montgomery. The crew is convinced she's a boy, and she hopes it stays that way until she has the chance to avenge the deaths of her mother and brother at the hands of the crew. All goes well until the ship takes a handsome captive. Could her feelings for him ruin her charade?

Sebastian Whitley is a young man in love. He sails on his father's ship, trying to find the beautiful girl he's lost. When he's captured by *The Bloody Maiden*, the annoying cabin boy saves his life – and makes it more difficult at the same time. His savior is actually a girl, and if Sebastian doesn't keep quiet, it could mean both their deaths.

Together, they have to thwart a mutiny, get revenge, and get off the ship before Alex's secret is revealed. If not, it's the plank for both of them.

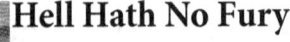

Also Available from Dragon's Roost Press

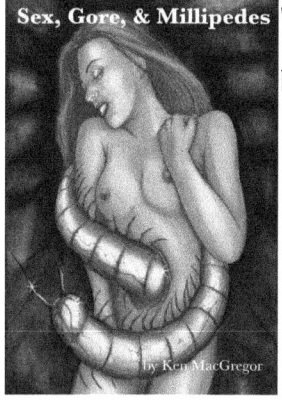

Sex, Gore, and Millipedes

by Ken MacGregor

Ken MacGregor, known for pushing boundaries in horror, for shoving the reader outside of their comfort zone, has finally gone too far. *Sex, Gore, and Millipedes* is a collection of the sickest stuff you've ever read. This book will hit your triggers. Hopefully, all of them. You've been warned.